Description

In this fantasy story Pendal, the NighT Guardian 's daughter, has moved on from her comfortable home beside the River Ohm. She has explored other regions, visited Cavahn 's monastery, and explored her spirituality by becoming a priest of Cavahn's order in addition to her own, Garfan monastic order. She is recognized as a Female warrior and Blade Smith. She journeys to the VodaKhan region intent on saving her mother from Assassination. She is revealed as the Dekar-na Empress, the ruler to replace the Emperor. This is book three in the NighT Guardian Series, click on the link to purchase and immerse yourself in the adventure.

I0664712

The NighT Guardian Book 3 – Blade Smith

Pendal held the breakfast bowl close to her face so that she could enjoy the warm spicy, nourishing smell of the food. She had just purchased it from the transport guardian who was brought a large steaming pot of it through the transport carriages and selling it the passengers.

This bowl of nourishing cereal, so different from the bowls of ground and spiced roots she had been brought up on was just one of the many new things she had experienced over the last two periods.

When Lovan said she had to leave the prison that day and told her she would be going on a long journey, she had never understood the magnitude of what he had meant. Or how long ago it seemed to be now. Pendal looked out of the transport's window at the world, a new world passing by. Tall cone shaped trees, deep passes with violent turbulent rivers flowing at their bottom. Snow, yes, for the first time she had seen, walked in and tasted snow! The NighT Guardian had described it at the table before she left but she could not imagine it until she saw it and touched it.

She had also never experienced cold the way it was here. Even in Mid Day Rise it was cold here. She had warm clothing, a head covering and her boots were more than a match for the weather, and she had to experiment with hand coverings. She had only worn them at the monastery when she was first out in the plantings. After a while they had acquired holes and she had stopped wearing them and not asked for replacements, preferring instead to feel the ground soil between her fingers; her hands had become rough as a result. She had only started wearing them again when she started blade training.

Her blade trainer demanded that her hands be less worn, calloused and the skin less broken from cuts and gouges. She had nothing against hard work and the evidence of it but to hold a blade and wear the handle so that it fitted the hand like it was born to the holder required hands in better condition than Pendal's.

And so it was that Pendal had gone back to wearing hand coverings and replacing them regularly. Her hands had improved and she did indeed feel she could hold a blade better without callouses, cuts and other accidents that happened out in the plantings under Moon Rise.

For a moment Pendal felt intensely sad. She wondered what had happened to the herbs she had left behind half way through their cycle of growth. Had the supplicant who took over from her been as loving and tender as she? Had the plantings been watered and fed growth nutrients to make them strong and healthy? She thought of the ground animals she played with when she had time out in the far plantings, would they be looking for their friend to play with and find her missing and be as sad as she was?

It was a way of life Pendal had left behind but knew she could fall back into quite easily. But for now, other things drove her, things that had brought her into the mountains of VodaKhan.

After leaving the prison, or battle castle, depending on your perspective, she had gone home with the NighT Guardian and with Cavahn had talked through what remained of Moon Rise and well into the next Day Rise when Vella had joined them.

Cavahn did not know of Pendal when she joined with the NighT Guardian but suspected he was her father from when she had first arrived. For the NighT Guardian, he had never seen Pendal grown; he had only seen her as a baby, just out of the womb. As far as he knew, he had spent more time with Pendal as a baby arranging the transaction to the monastery than the Empress who had birthed her.

Then there was the question of how old she was, twenty-two cycles, twenty-three, or maybe even twenty-four. Age was not counted by the actual number of Day Rises in a period or the number of periods in a cycle; it included a correction according to the study cycle in to which a growing child would be schooled by educators, and corrected again by the number of day risings in that period. Some periods were longer than others depending on the rotation of the world. Pendal didn't know how old she was because the monastery was not required to follow the adjustments and corrections of the outside world. Pendal really didn't care, if she ever met someone who needed to know, they would calculate her age then.

However, it was interesting to see Vella who had treated her as a younger sister realize that Pendal was the older of all of them.

Pendal sipped at the warm breakfast cereal until she needed a utensil to get the thicker pieces into her mouth.

Always her eyes scanned the other riders in the transport, noting who had changed position, who had finished their cereal and who did not buy any food.

She did not sit in one of the seats in the middle of the carriage, rather she sat in a seat attached to the wall of the carriage, which meant no one was sitting behind her and careful location of her thick over cloak and her pack stopped anyone sitting opposite her or beside her. The exit from the carriage was to her left and allowed her easy escape if needed into to another carriage; to her right was a special window that popped out allowing escape in the event of an accident, but of course, it could also be used to allow someone to escape a personal threat.

Unlike a lot of people on the transport, Pendal wore her boots almost all the time. In the event of a threat she had to escape from, there would be little time to put on her boots. The boots were the same ones she walked from the monastery to her home. Before she left The NighT Guardian had insisted on taking them in to the boot maker in the village to have some additional animal skin and decoration added as a gift, he also wanted the soles to be repaired and generally to be in good order for the journey she was to undertake.

When he returned she was extremely pleased with the repairs and the added decoration. She hugged her father deeply and dearly. He had hugged her equally affectionately and then shown her the value of the added features he had the boot maker include. The decoration allowed for extra space in which to hide an additional blade. He then presented her with a pair of unique blades. He explained they were his father's; they were the blades of an assassin his father had confronted and killed before the ma could use them on his target.

Smaller, they were intended for throwing not a hand contest, the blades were designed to maximize damage to an intended target. Razor sharp they would cut into a target extremely easily. They had backward pointing notches that would tear flesh as the blade was removed. The only way to avoid making the wound worse from the blade's notches and tearing was to cut a wider and deeper wound around the blade and remove it that way. Whether you cut a bigger wound or pulled the blade out with no regard for the tearing of flesh, the victim would be substantially worse off and likely die from the weapon's extraction if not the initial delivery.

Now with her main blade on show, a blade at her back and a throwing blade in each boot and one in her pack, she carried a total of five blades and she was extremely proficient with all of them. She was a Cavahn put it, a Blade Smith.

As Pendal looked out of the window, she continued eating her wonderful breakfast. The gentle swaying of the transport as it moved along metal bars locked into the ground lulled Pendal into reflection of the past two periods.

Although it was clear now who her father and mother were, and that she was part of the Imperial bloodline, it was around the table on the verandah that she felt most at ease, most loved and cared for and for the first time in her life, supported in what she wanted and needed to do in and with her life. The idea of running out and killing the Emperor as her mother would like her to do and assume the role of Empress was as remote a thought as what was to follow that Moon Rise, now so long ago, when the priests pulled her out of her cot, stripped her and marched her naked to the High Priest's office and locked her inside.

It was Pendal that decided her safest place was out in the wider lands, to leave home, the village, and her family down by the river and travel, to see the entire region and as many of the others as she could. It was a practical decision not made with the heart but the analytical mind and help of her more business-like guardian spirit who watched over her. It would mean the family would not know where she was but, she reasoned, and they agreed nether would anyone purposefully looking for her. Like a wandering healer, she had left home, that sweet house down by the river, with the swaying reeds and the mischievous ground animals and headed away from the valley, away from the River Ohm.

She had travelled East, South and then to the Deep South west, and then turned north and further west. She passed through lands and regions she had only heard of when sitting like a child at the knee of her father as he recounted stories of his adventures. She had passed through lands The NighT Guardian had campaigned in, and many he had not.

One of the most important places and the last before her big adventure was Cavahn's monastery, the monastery of the order of 1. Cavahn had given her instructions and a letter of introduction to the High Priest. Through all the places she visited she anticipated her stay at the monastery to be the most delicious of all.

It had not disappointed.

She had spent sixteen Day Rises there, studying, training in new techniques and fighting arts; she reveled in them as she did conversation at the communal dinning room table with supplicants and priests. She spent time in the plantings under Moon Rise, tending the precious night flowering herbs. When she finally left they had captured her heart and they had made her a priest, around her neck and her left wrist she wore the sacred emblems of the priest hood.

It was at the monastery that the High Priest suggested an adventure that Pendal had not even considered. It was suggested that Pendal take a voyage on one of the great sailing ships that left harbour in a nearby coastal town. Pendal was to experience the lands and places on the far side of the Great Salt Sea. In her mind she heard a voice, the voice of a spirit speaking telling her this was a good idea, a sound idea, and one she needed to take action on. It was the voice of her other guardian sprit that was not often heard but one she listened to this time.

As Pendal looked out of the window of the transport she could see fresh snow on the taller trees and down in the valley. The white snow reminded her of the white foam on the crests of the waves as the great ship left harbour. That day the ships sails were filled with wind like a great belly filled with food at a celebration.

So much was new to her, she had never had anything but soil under her feet and between her toes but on the ship there was just the wood of the deck, and like the great bed up stairs on the second verandah, the hammock they called it on a ship, rocked her gently to sleep. The Moons seemed so much clearer and brighter out on the Great Salt Sea and the smaller bright lights in the night sky shone brighter lighting her way.

As a priest, she gained special attention from all on the ship, and the leader of the ship who was called a captain, taught her simple navigation by the stars showing her how they lined the ship up with one star and on the next Moon Rise, with another. He showed her the delicate instruments they used to find their way when the sky was angry and hid the moon and stars from sight.

She had stood holding tightly to the rail as the ship rocked and rolled in a violent storm and with her face wet with liquid and her lips tasting of salt she had breathed in an experience very, very few people in the towns and villages she had passed through would ever comprehend. And at the next Day Rise, she marveled at how the liquid of the Salt Sea had been clear and smooth like glass yet had been so violent during the storm.

When the great sailing ship tied itself to the harbour in a far off land Pendal could not wait to experience the harbour, its people and life in this new land to her. She stepped off the boards placed for travellers and crew to get off and on the ship with the slightest of doubt that land on this side of the Salt Sea was the same as what she had left.

The sounds and smells, the tastes and the words spoken and how they were spoken were so strange to her. This really was something new and exciting, it was intoxicating and there was a sense of danger and risk to everything she saw.

In the town she had stopped and looked around for a liquid seller to buy something to drink for her thirst. The bowl given to her had beautiful pink and blue flowers resting on the fluid surface. She saw another from the ship stop and buy a bowl of the same liquid with the same beautiful scented flowers and watched them as they tried to eat the flowers to the loud humor of the liquid seller. Pendal thought "good to know" don't eat the flowers. Not that she would, she recognized the scent of the blue one as being similar to one of the night flowering herbs that she was used to tend. The Liquid had a fragrant smell and a wonderful mild taste to it that was pleasing both the nose and the tongue. It was refreshing and stimulated her to explore further.

Soon she found herself on a hill top overlooking the harbour, she could see the colourfully painted homes and businesses of the townsfolk, the roads bringing goods and people into and out of the town, the monastery across the harbour and the large sailing ship that brought her here tied to the harbour wall. A myriad of smaller sailboats for moving across the harbour and for pleasure dotted the protected harbour space. Far to her left she could see a river entering its liquid into the harbour and the Salt Sea. As she sat under a Mid Day Rise that did not require the wearing of heavy protective cloaks for some reason, she felt the warm winds from inland moving to join those already on the Great Salt Sea, and then the change of direction as the cooler ones from the Great Sea come inland.

It was restful, joyful, exciting and she wished she could stay.
Pendal could only stay in the land across the Great Salt Sea for as long as the great sailing ship remained in harbour off loading the goods it had brought, and taking on new cargo. Two, perhaps Three Day Rises was all the time she had there, but it was an exciting and reveling time as she watched the pace and earnest industry of the people in this strange land. It was a land she would like to have spent more time in and to learn the language, in the short time there she had already learned enough to allow her to order a tasty meal of roasted ground vegetables, and a white fleshed sea creature.

The return across the Salt Sea was calm and uneventful, and with strong winds from the land they had just left the sailing ship made good time. Pendal spent every moment she could under Moon Rise on the deck of the ship looking at the moons, the stars and the playful sea creatures pacing the sailing ship on its journey.

Pendal was sitting at the front of the ship, the bow they called it, when the captain came to her and announced that next Day Rise they would be stopping at a Northern VodaKhan port. As requested in the terms of her voyage, she was to leave the ship, they would be collecting more cargo, but their time in port would be a short one, she should be ready to leave the ship as soon as it was tied to the harbour.

As Pendal threw the last of her food scraps to a sea creature swimming alongside the ship she rested her hands on the side of the ship and her chin on the back of her hands and for the first time on her journey, she was genuinely sad. This had been more than a simple voyage on the journey of her life; it had been a time when she had not had to place a hand on a blade, though she knew where they were at all times and made sure they were available if required. That last night on the Great Sailing ship allowed her to close her thoughts and free her mind, she prepared for the world she was returning to, the world of the Emperor and all the dark clouds that surrounded him.

The ship arrived at the VodaKhan harbour and was tied to the harbour wall just after first Day Rise. Pendal was standing on the deck of the ship with her pack, her cloak tight around her neck, under the clasps that closed it, her badge of office. As she walked down the planking's she could see to her right and left small well guarded and heavily covered carts ready to load what she knew from Lovan was VodaKhan gold.

Unlike the warm breezes she felt on the hillside of the far off harbour, here a cool wind was blowing that seemed much colder than she knew it to be from the captain. The houses and business premises she could see were not brightly painted, here they were left bare or painted a dark brown or even black. It was not an inviting place.

To Pendal it was a necessity she leave the ship and move inland. She had discussed being in the interior of VodaKhan with Vella and the NighT Guardian before she left home but not how she would get there or that she should come across the Great Salt Sea. Her destiny lay in what happened in VodaKhan, and here she was.

As she walked between the heavily covered carts she encountered a ring of VodaKhan troops and a Guard Captain about her height, he was well protected with body armour and carried several blades at his waist. Pendal examined his gate and his stance. He may carry main blades but he was unlikely to use them well. There was a slight limp and the armour seemed too tight on the side the blade handles pointed to, the tight armour would not allow him the flexibility he would need in a fight. She considered his other hand but again surmised he was not adept with that either as there was three fingers missing. Of course Pendal knew not to make decisions based on what she surmised, until she was actually in a fight him, she would not know for certain if she were right or wrong.

He held up his blade hand indicating she should stop!

Using his blade hand for communication placed his hand even further away from the handles of his multiple blades. Nevertheless, her blade hand was at the ready under her cloak, resting on the handle.

With her other hand she held out her Badge of Office from between the folds of her cloak.

He studied it.

Then he pointed to a much older man several feet away who was watching Pendal and the Guard Captain. He stood slightly bent over with a stick for support, he had a broad chest and body, he had thick dark hair and thick, heavy eye brows that reminded Pendal of the crawling creatures that ate the leaves of the night flowering herbs she used to tend. The creatures had to be collected and thrown in a decorative lake of river creatures in the monastery gardens. The river creatures loved them and would fight each other to eat the best of them.

As she neared him, she could see his face, the skin was old and deeply folded, for a moment Pendal thought the face was to big for his skull and had been attached only at certain points, leaving the rest to hang loosely. But no, this was his real face. The eyes were a liquid blue but looked tired and worn. The corners of his mouth drooped. Instead of a cloak, he had a thick coat that looked like it had been made from multiple animal skins.

As she walked up to him with the Captain in tow, she started to bring out her Badge of Office out from under her cloak but the man waved it away with a boney hand, "I am Oskar, Chief Protector of this Quadrant," the voice was deep and seemed to echo from somewhere inside is broad chest. "Welcome to VodaKhan, Bashar Pendal." While making the welcoming statement he waved the Guard Captain away.

For a long moment, Pendal and Oskar regarded each other. It was Pendal who broke the silence, "Are we to be adversaries, or, friends?" she asked.

Oskar studied Pendal for what seemed to be an eternity; around them the sounds of the harbour workers loading the VodaKhan gold on to the sailing ship seemed to be dull and remote. The shouts of the sailors as they started to set the sails for leaving harbour only just made more noise than the dockworkers.

Pendal waited.

"When you sat on the hill overlooking the harbour across the Great Salt Sea, how did you find the wind?" Oskar asked.

"Playful" was Pendal's response. Maybe it was one of her guiding spirits talking to her but Pendal did not think the question odd nor her response to it.

"I to found it playful. It was a long time ago that I sat on that hill." Oskar looked down at his feet for a moment and then looked back into Pendal's eyes, "we shall be friends!" he exclaimed. He half turned and pointed with his stick down the path by the harbour, Pendal could see another group of soldiers and a conveyance pulled by two horses. "Tell me, are the houses brightly colourful?"

Pendal walked beside him, matching the old mans pace. "Yes, surprisingly so. The houses in all the regions I have visited are dull in comparison. I would like to go back and spend some time there." What Pendal said next was a revelation to her, "I think I could be happy there."

Oskar's stick made clicking sounds on the hard stone of the harbour, "yes, that is the sentiment I have of that harbour as well. Maybe I will" he responded. "It was a long time ago, that I visited there, I stood up straight then and was not bent over. It was a time a little like you have had, a time of travel and a time of relaxation and pleasure for the soul. I came back and joined the Guard, and the rest is history as they say." Oskar did not look at Pendal as he spoke, but she felt it was revealing and something he had not shared with anyone.

"It was a time in clear Day Rise when I did not need a heavy cloak to protect me, and the warm winds off the land and the cool ones of the Great Salt Sea exchanged and played with the long grasses and my hair" said Pendal. "I would liked to have taken food and river liquid and sat out for a long time." Then, thinking of her experience on the hill that day she said, "Perhaps it would have been nice to take a bedroll and slept out there. Under the stars, and watch the moons rise."

Oskar stopped and turned to Pendal and looked deeply into her eyes but did not say anything; he turned and continued walking in silence.

Before they reached the conveyance, Oskar stopped again and turned to look at Pendal, "yes, indeed we will be friends" and he reached out and touched her arm, "yes, we will be friends" he repeated.

The ride in the conveyance was surprisingly relaxing as it slowly took them through the streets of the harbour and out along a road beside the Salt Sea to a complex of low buildings hugging an upward curve in the coast line that formed rocky cliffs. As Pendal looked out, she could already see the Great Sailing Ship that had brought her here but first it had taken across the Great Salt Sea to that hill that now allowed her to be friends with what she felt could have been a lethal adversary.

Pendal was under no illusion that Oskar for all his bent over age, stick, and old, worn face had a very shrewd and powerful mind and the rank to carry out his wishes. Every VodaKhan guard they met, no matter of what rank was immediately deferential to Oskar the moment they saw him, perhaps Pendal thought, his power was greater than just the quadrant of which he said he was the protector. She was also under no illusion that the expression of words of friendship was no substitute for demonstrating it, and that had not happened yet.

They went directly to Oskar's official office.

It was very large.

It was powerful.

Glass on three sides, on ne side looking out over the Salt Sea, she could see her ship was already well out from land and headed away to its homeport where she had joined it. From anther side she could see the harbour and the protected water for ships, on the third side she could see roads and swirling trees and very long grasses.

The clouds were clearing and Day Rise was starting to illuminate this land and turn the colours bright and vibrant, but not so vibrant as those she saw from on top of that hill.

She heard Oskar set his weight into a large chair behind a spacious desk. Opposite the desk were four comfortable chairs, he must be here late she realized as the place had an abundance of lighting globes, on the desk, and the fourth wall, and high in the celling. There was a long table, black and highly polished for meetings and conferences, Pendal counted seats, ten on each side and two at the far end, just one large spacious chair at the other, the one Oskar sat in she thought.

As she looked around the office and at his desk, Pendal noted the lack of paper or books to record information and make it available to others. Then a voice in her head said to Pendal "he plans, and puts others in motion, he does not move, Oskar is power."

Pendal placed her backpack and a robe on one of the chairs facing Oskar across his desk and sat down. As she did, she took off her badge of office and carefully folded the cord and placed it in its case in her backpack.

As she sat and looked across at Oskar she was aware of how true those words were, there were few personal mementos of journeys taken, family, events in his life that he wanted to be reminded of. Even Pendal had a few, a very few treasured possessions from her time at the monastery where she grew up, her departure that last night had been delayed as a priest had been sent to her room to collect them.

Pendal became aware of a red animal skin covered box in front of her. It had not been there when she first entered and scanned the room. Oskar must have put it there when she was looking out of the windows or taking note of his office.

"It is for you!" said Oskar. "The Imperial Badge of Office you have will not get you very far in VodaKhan."

Pendal reached for the box as she did she saw her hand perfectly reflected in the surface of the desk, it was much more highly polished than she had expected; she stopped reaching for the box and touched the surface of it. It looked like wood but now as she ran her hand over it, it felt like polished stone.

"Wood stone" smiled Oskar. "You do not have it in the lower regions. Ancient trees pressed and shaped by great forces underground turn the wood to stone. The conference table is one piece; it took fifty men to get it in and set up, the windows had to be taken out, all of them."

Pendal continued to reach for the box, took and opened it.

"Think of it as a key," said Oskar. The tone of his voice changed to one that seemed to carry great weight and demanded attention.

Inside a round solid metal rod about the width of two fingers and the length of her longest middle finger, at the top a beautifully made maroon rope to wear this key around her neck. She ran her fingers over the material.

It was material from her Garfan robe!

Pendal silently and without showing it took a deep breath to allow the surprise to dissipate into the world. How and where they had managed to acquire the material she could not comprehend. Pendal took another silent deep breath and expelled it slowly allowing it to clear the last of her worry at seeing it.

Pendal slipped the metal rod out, around the top of the rod was repeated four times a bird of prey holding a shield which Pendal recognized as being the VodaKhan battle shield. It seemed to be everywhere there was some official presence. It had been on the conveyance they came in and it was on buckles on the elaborate animal skin harness that joined the horses to the conveyance. It had been on the carts carrying the VodaKhan gold at the harbour and on a few buildings close to where the sailing ship was docked. She saw it on the uniform of every soldier.

The animal's foot claws held the shield at its base and it's wing claws held the shield at the top. The head with the flesh-cutting beak was three headed, one head looking to the left, one to the right and one directly at you. Below, running up and down the rod and around it was writing, and numerous symbols, she did not recognize most of them, but some she did. They were the same as those on her Imperial Badge of Office. The symbols were from the two archaic languages used at the Imperial Court, and in a recessed and intricately framed area, her name in those two languages plus VodaKhan. Before she left Cavahn's monastery, and knowing she would be going to VodaKhan territory, they had taught her to recognize and write her name in VodaKhan symbols.

She felt something inscribed on the bottom, she turned it up so she could see. At the bottom of the rod, the same representation of the bird of Prey and the VodaKhan battle shield engraved in beautiful detail.

The rod was heavy.

Pendal holds it in her hand as if weighing it, it is not just the bar that Pendal was weighing, she was also weighing how Oskar was viewing her, trying to decide from the close attention whether he can be prompted to action and provide information without being asked directly. As she continued testing and observing Oskar she transferred the bar to her other hand to continue assessing its weight, she would also like to know from what metal it is made, she had never seen this metal before.

"The bar is made from white gold. It is from mines in the very far north where snow and ice hundreds of feet thick covers the ground year round." Oskar cleared his throat, "if you wish I can arrange for you to see the land and the mine," he said. "If you wanted to go you would be the first non VodaKhan to see it."

Pendal looked up into those old blue eyes, so, she thought, valuable information, he is proud of the material this bar is made from and the fact he can arrange for a non-VodaKhan to see its source. "I would like that," said Pendal in response. She now knew she could acquire information from him without asking by the sue of her actions and suspenseful time.

Pendal was sure the game of observer observing the observed, he to her, and her to him would continue through their "friendship."

"I was told my Imperial Badge of Office, would guarantee me freedom of movement in all the lands the Emperor rules over," Pendal said. "I am happy to use this key in VodaKhan lands. Does it guarantee me freedom of movement?" Pendal asked.

Oskar stares at her without moving, or answering, after a few moments he makes a sucking sound through his teeth. Meeting Pendal's gaze directly, "It would not be wise to display your Imperial rank in VodaKhan, yes the region is part of the empire but the Emperor does not, and cannot enforce his will here. I am sure you know it is VodaKhan gold that allows the Emperor to rule. If he did not receive our gold for his lavish expenses, everyone in the lower regions would be taxed until they walked around in rags." Oskar stared out of the window, and nodded. Pendal followed his gaze and; the ship Pendal had arrived on was well out of harbour and on its way to its homeport.

"You should know that while you were on the ship," Oskar continued to stare at the ship as the sails filled with wind and the bow started to make bigger white waves as it cut through the Salt Sea. "The Emperor moved against Sovan, Sovan is dead, executed for treason, theft, and rape. The emperor is actively hunting for the Empress but has not found her." Oskar turned back to look at Pendal, "Your mother is on VodaKhan territory."

"But she is not safe" said Pendal meeting Oskar's gaze.

Oskar made the sucking sound through his teeth for a second time as he regarded how efficiently Pendal had understood that the missing word "safe" from his sentence was not a casual mistake but had meaning. "No, she is not safe. Imperial Agents operate in her location, we are moving to help her as quickly as we can but those agents have slowed us. We have lost contact with her location."

Silence.

Oskar's eyes looks misty, vacant, inwardly Pendal realizes, his mind is working on the problem, perhaps many connected with the safety of her mother. As Oskar works on his problem, Pendal's mind starts to float off on hers. The Empress remains in danger, and yes she does think of her as her mother, she can express concern her but there is no emotional connection to the Empress yet and probably never will have as a mother. The Empress played no part in Pendal's growing up.

There is a knock at the door someone is waiting to enter.

Oskar and Pendal's eyes return from the world of thought to the world of physical existence and stare at each other. Their minds refocus on the present.

Oskar raises himself from his chair and slowly, stiffly walks around to Pendal's side of the desk. He gently takes the decorated rod from her hand. "Protocol" he says quietly. "At the long table you will stand to my right side and I will hold this in front of you. You will take this from me with your l left hand. I will announce your name and you will sit at my right hand. If there is someone at that seat, they must move." Oskar looked up at the door and waited for a moment as the knocking was repeated. "There is usually a Lieutenant Colonel who takes the seat at my right hand. He is arrogant and stupid, he is aggressive to those of equal rank and a like an untrained vanmor savaging those under him. If I have few friends, he has none. He sits there only from habit and because no one has displaced him. His habit will be broken by you." Oskar paused, "he is an Imperial Agent. The Emperor uses our gold to buy his allegiance and his soul." Oskar looked thoughtful, "everyone at the table knows, we feed him disinformation so he will pass it to his master, important decisions are made without him." Oskar looked down at the blade at Pendal's waist, "I am aware you carry two blades, one at the front on display and with which you are very, very proficient. Under your robes, you carry one at your back, which is extremely unusual. Please, do me the honour of showing both. If he challenges you, kill him!"

Pendal looked at the old man for a long moment and then nodded.

The knocking at the door was repeated; this time the number of knocks was increased, adding some urgency and insistence that the person outside is allowed to enter. Oskar gestured for Pendal to follow him to the long table, as she rose from her seat, Pendal shrugged off her long outer robe revealing the arrangement of belts and sheaths that kept both blades in place and the back one especially out of sight. It was a gift from her father the NighT Guardian. He made it for her before she left home after seeing the arrangement she had created for herself. This was streamlined and held both blades perfectly.

As Pendal followed Oskar to the long table he rapped on the floor with his stick several times, a signal to who was outside that they could enter.

What entered surprised Pendal, she counted eighteen officers, some male, and some female. Some in light battle armour some, dressed in more formal attire. They all regarded her with interest but in front of Oskar would not express any surprise. Each stood patiently behind a chair waiting the order to sit. The seats at the far end were empty. The last to enter was a slightly less than middle aged officer, with short dark trimmed hair, a beautifully detailed uniform, brightly shined shoes and an elaborate belt arrangement that supported a single blade, the sheath for the blade had a relief cut out to show the blade had been gilded with gold and engraved with a VodaKhan shield but with no bird of prey.

As Oskar had described he held the rod in front of Pendal and announced her name. Around the table the officers repeated her name. The officer standing behind the chair where Pendal knew she was to sit simply made the motion of a cough without repeating her name. Oskar gave the rod to Pendal and as he had said, and he announced she would sit at his right hand. As Pendal watched the officers on the right side moved down one seat with the furthest officer moving around to take a seat at the end.

The officer standing to the right of Oskar's seat did not move instead he looked angrily at Oskar and with hate at Pendal. The seat to his right was now vacant for him but he did not move to stand behind it.

Pendal took a step forward and placed the rod she had received on the table in front of where she would sit, Pendal stood within an arms length of the officer and placed a hand on the high back of the chair. "I sit here, not you" she said quietly but firmly. Pendal's position was now much closer, well within the strike range of his right blade hand.

Pendal saw a crease in the right arm of the officers uniform suddenly flex. Within a moment she had taken a giant leap backwards away from the chair and the officer. He pushed the chair violently towards the table to make way for his thrusting right hand and blade. If Pendal had not moved backwards so violently, the blade would have been in her body just below her right breast.

Her front bade was drawn silently and brought upwards to parry a scything sweep of the officer's blade intended for the left side of her head and shoulder. Pendal raised up on her right foot and pivoted inward and at the same time away from the officer in a gentle arc she had learned dancing at the Garfan monastery for the delight of guests who were there to purchase a surrogate son or daughter. She had always enjoyed the grace and athleticism of the move, in this blade fight it was unexpected and allowed Pendal to slash at the underarm of the officers left arm. Instead of skin and bone, Pendal's blade touched body armour and left no potential lethal cut.

The officer made a grunt of pleasure and grasped the chair, and turned it on its side with the high back pointed across Pendal's path, it was intended as a block to further moves by Pendal on his left side. Pendal did not react, to react in surprise or try and create a strategy to deal with what had occurred would slow her mind and divert its attention from her mission.

Pendal used the high back of the chair as leverage to leap over it and place herself on his right side. Doing so surprised the officer; he had not expected his opponent to place herself on the side he was armed. He had expected her to stay on the other side of the obstacle. As Pendal moved over the chair, she twisted it, bringing it closer to his left leg. As she landed, she brought her blade up to parry a wild slashing movement by the officer.

Pendal continued her move to his blade side, which forced him to twist and turn to remain facing her, as he did, his foot caught on the high back of the chair where Pendal had moved it. He twisted to his left to free his foot and jump over the chair, but in doing so, he stumbled and bent over exposing the back of his neck.

Pendal reached behind her and grasped her second blade, it unsheathed silently and she brought it up in a tight arc along the officers back and she drove it into the back of his neck and into his brain. She twisted the blade to sever the spine from the skull. The officer was dead before his face touched the floor.

Pendal took two steps back from the fallen officer and the table, a blade in each hand. She looked around the table and at Oskar who was starting to smile. There was no movement toward her but clearly some of those standing at the table were relieved at the outcome.
It was the first time Pendal had killed in a blade fight and she took a moment to thank her guiding spirits and in the physical world, Cavahn. She took a moment to wish the spirit of the officer would find it's place in the afterlife and not dwell as a wandering spirit in this one.

Before she left home a series or brutal training sessions with Cavahn had emphasized her understanding of the goal of a blade fight. Drawing out a fight by nicking an opponent repeatedly so they bled slowly and were weakened over the contest to show off your skills to judges was gone. Endurance was useful in a blade fight but was not a goal. She had learned that a blade fight must end quickly, within seconds of it starting and the ending must be with the opponent dead.

Pendal had studied with Cavahn the locations of vital organs and how to end an opponent by attacking those, which added to the lack of surprise Pendal had felt at finding armour where she thought she would wound the officer. The back of the neck at the base of the skull and severing the spine were two things she had brought together in this fight which Cavahn had taught her separately.

As the last officer past through the door and closed it after him, Pendal turned to look at Oskar, "Do all meetings start with a killing?" she asked. After the officer lay dead on the floor there was only a few short moments before the closest two officers had moved to carry the body out of the room, and, almost on queue, two juniors entered to clean up the floor and with Pendal's approval her blade and her hand, both had blood on them. The chair turned out to have a damaged leg and was replaced.

Through out all of this Oskar and the other officers remained standing at their designated seats. A short meeting had been convened after all the cleaning and repairs, it had been mostly about what the deceased spy might have passed or not to the Emperor. Plans had been made to send misleading information to the south and they had to know whether the information got to its intended destination.

Then the meeting had ended.

Oskar appeared to roll back into his seat behind his desk; Pendal sat on the ledge of the window that looked out over the harbour, her feet swinging free of the floor.

As Oskar struggled to make himself comfortable he replied, "no they do not," he grunted as he pulled an offending cushion out from behind his back and threw it on the floor. "Apart from his brutality to juniors and his arrogance to his peers, keeping an Imperial Spy close so misleading information can be sent through them to its destination was becoming burdensome."

Pendal looked at her boots and tapped the toes together, "then why did you allow him to stay. Even if he was not an Imperial spy, it sounds as if his qualities did not merit his position at your right hand? She asked.

Oskar considered her for a moment, "have you heard the expression, keep your friends close, your enemies closer and closest of all, dead enemies?" he said.

"No, I have not" replied Pendal. "The meeting" said Pendal, returning to the subject following the demise of the officer. "The reports I was most interested in concerned the whereabouts of the Empress. When will there be new reports?" she asked.

There was a knock at the door followed by three officers who had been at the meeting and had been instructed to return after they left to make agreed on preparations. They were clearly unaccustomed to seeing cushions thrown on the floor and such a high-ranking quest as Pendal sitting on a ledge by one of the windows, swinging her legs like a child at her dinner table stool.

"Pendal" said Oskar, "these three officers will arrange for you to have the best and lightest body armour we can produce. I will not let you go out searching for the Empress in a region that has the most Imperial spies. As your friend I ask you to take protection." The word 'friend' seemed to cause shock amongst the three officers, which Pendal registered but did not respond to, clearly, for Oskar to use the word was strange and created confusion.

Pendal jumped down from the ledge, landing silently on both feet even though she was wearing her heavy boots. "Oskar, your friend here, as you have seen, can take care of herself" she afforded him a beaming smile.

Oskar leaned forward, partially resting on his desk, "give some comfort to an old man and at least have some body armour fitted?" the conversation was starting to have a warmth that oddly was not unexpected.

Pendal moved to the chair at Oskar's desk where her cloak and pack rested, she placed the case with her new key inside in the pack and picked them both up. Then, as an act of inspiration and from a voice of one of her guiding sprits she walked around to Oskar's side of the desk and gave the old man a hug and a kiss on the cheek. Oskar stood and returned her hug and kiss.

As Pendal moved swiftly back around Oskar's table, the three officers took two steps backward. What they had just witnessed was so out of character for Oskar that Pendal was sure the story would be told over and over again in the mess and met with the same incredulity at each telling.

Pendal stopped by one of the chairs in front of Oskar's desk. A soft voice spoke to her it told her to take the help offered. She turned to Oskar, "If is am going searching for a valuable person in a nest of Imperial spies and not wait for more reports, I suppose I do need some extra help, the armour is most welcome, thank you," she said. Oskar and Pendal nodded to each other. Pendal turned and left with the officers.

Pendal studied several new people that had come into the carriage. What appeared to be parents and two children, the mother was carrying a sleeping baby, and there was a very bored boy about fourteen cycles. He carried a small tube normally used for sending reading material, papers, and other similar things via courier. He had writing instruments in his hands and a small board for holding study papers. As he sat, bored in the corner of his seat chewing like some farm animal, he faced Pendal. The husband sat with his back to Pendal, she could only see part of his right shoulder and the side of his head. There was little discourse between them. The group was unusually silent, even the baby was silent and unmoving, not even gurgling sounds from happy sleeping could be heard.

Pendal took the last mouthful of her breakfast and set the bowl down on a small window table. She placed her feet firmly in the floor of the carriage. The fine body armour Oskar's people had made for her moved effortlessly with her body and outwardly showed no evidence it existed.

Pendal leaned forward to adjust her robe and better position her thigh and foreleg armour. As she did she shrugged her shoulders out of her heavy robe. Her back blade was still covered and secret she carefully touched the handle to assure her it moved freely. She reached forward and her fingers slipped in to the decorative covers of her boots to check the throwing knives her father had gifted her with. They moved easily in their holders, with her heavy robe off her shoulders Pendal was able to move freely. She still marveled that the body armour did not show that she was wearing it.

Looking around the corner of her seat Pendal could see an older woman being helped into her seat by a dotting son and his wife. Pendal could not see the woman's face clearly but she heard the woman's voice groan as she sat down and her weight was taken off her poor legs. The son and his wife busied themselves putting their traveling luggage in the overhead carrying racks. There was a pillow for the old woman's head and the son's wife had just placed a sleeping blanket over the woman to keep her warm. The son was standing struggling with the window latch; he wanted to release it to allow cool clean air in from outside.

Turning back to where she sat, Pendal looked out of the window at some spectacular liquid falls. The river she could see wound its way around several outcroppings and then the land simply stopped, leaving the river liquid to cascade in two huge falls that appeared to compete for the amount of liquid they put onto the rocks below. The pounding sound of the liquid on the rocks was impressive.

A voice inside Pendal's head told her to turn around immediately. Pendal had come to respect and obey these voices in her head; they were the voices of her guiding spirits and they had never been wrong.

As she looked around he boy was taking something he had been chewing out of his mouth and wrapping it around the end of one of his writing instruments, on his lap rested the small tube, Pendal instantly recognized the combination materials as a breath pipe.

The boy's mother who was acting as a lookout for someone almost certainly not her son spoke sharply and loudly to the boy, he looked up and saw that Pendal had seen what he was doing.

Pendal reached across her body and picked up the breakfast bowl from the window table and threw it left-handed at the boy. The combination of trying to jam the writing instrument that Pendal could now see was a dart, and the chewing material into the small pipe while ducking the breakfast bowl made the boy fumble the device. Pendal jerked her right leg straight and held her hand near the top of her boot. The throwing blade slid out easily and into her hand. She wiped her arm back and threw the blade at the struggling boy.

The mother of the trio was starting to stand and throw the baby at Pendal. As her hands left the baby, one held the end of its wrapping cloth, which peeled off to reveal what she had thrown at Pendal.

It was disgusting, hairy and had horrible yellow and black stained teeth. Its hind legs claws bared were starting to come up under its body and it yellow front ripping claws were extended. It was a baby, a baby vanmor.

Pendal stood and rotated to the right so that her body was out of the direct path of the airborne animal. As she stood and moved, she took her back blade out and like the animal she and Vella had dispatched by the river with their pain sticks, she plunged the blade up into the animas belly as it passed by. Its front claws grasped for her forearm but slipped off the fine VodaKhan body armour under her robe. The animal landed where Pendal had been sitting and floundered on the seat dying.

The mother turned to look at her son, as she did she let out a shriek, her son was dead, Pendal's throwing blade buried up to the hilt in the soft space between his eyes. The mother turned back to Pendal spitting at her as she moved up and out of her seat with her blade held in a high guard position. She rushed toward Pendal.

Pendal ducked the blade slash but felt the thud of it on her back armour. She allowed the momentum of the woman to help turn her and bring her left blade up into the woman's throat. She fell lifeless on the still twitching body of the baby vanmor.

In the chaos, the father had started to get up form his seat but the mad attack by his wife had crossed his path and knocked him back down, he was now up and turning toward the far end of the carriage. Pendal reached for him but could only slash at his trailing leg. The cut across his lower leg made him scream and made it difficult for him to stand let alone walk or run. Hi leg started to drag behind him as he struggled to move forward.

A projectile weapon made a loud bang behind and to Pendal's left; the transport warden had come back into the carriage. The father of the murderous family jerked as the weapon's tiny missile entered his back. In the seats on the other side from where Pendal had been sitting, two men rose up and plunged their military issues blades into the man's chest.

Silence.

Pendal moved to the left, into the seats where the now dead family had been sitting. As she turned to face wherever a threat may come from she jerked the throwing blade out of the boys face.

Silence.

Then there was commotion at both ends of the carriage at the same time. Several VodaKhan officers entered whom Pendal remembered from the meeting. Then to her right a familiar sound of air being sucked between teeth. Oskar.

She looked up at her old friend and slowly relaxed and stood up straight, slowly sheathing her blades. Oskar studied the dead woman and the dead baby vanmor. He looked at the boy still seated with his breath tube on his lap. Then he moved forward to look at the deep wound on the man's trailing leg and the distance to the old woman and the son and daughter at the far end of the carriage.

Oskar turned to the carriage warden who was hiding his weapon back under his carriage warden's cloak. "Well done, well done."

Oskar gestured with his stick to the two men who had plunged their blades into the chest of the man who lay dead at their feet, "It is lucky we had Pendal, a blade smith here, I have little doubt she would have settled this one as well," Oskar prodded the corpse with his stick. "More training!" he exclaimed. "You must be faster and more attentive in future."

Oskar sucked in air between his teeth and looked at Pendal. "These two were supposed to be your protectors, assassins such as these three were not supposed to get close to you or your mother."

"My mother!" exclaimed Pendal. Oskar nodded, and with his stick pointed to the end of the carriage. Pendal came out to stand by Oskar, all she could see was an old woman sleeping peacefully and a son and daughter standing putting projectile weapons away in their clothing.

Pendal and Oskar stood beside the transport, its pulling engine snorting and sniffling at the front said that it wanted to get going and chaffed at the unscheduled stop. The carriage in which the attack had occurred was now the centre of four rings of heavily armed VodaKhan soldiers, and through each carriage in the transport traveling papers of each person were being examined by no less than a dozen of Oskar's agents.

They watched as several soldiers and the "son and daughter" traveling with the old lady disembarked with her on a carrying bed. Several healers waited beside the horse drawn carriage on which they would all continue their journey. The old lady was still quiet and sleeping.

"Imperial agents located your mother who was lightly guarded," Oskar stopped to make the now familiar if slightly disgusting sound of sucking air through his teeth. "The VodaKhan guards were killed and the Empress drugged. The Imperials intended to take her back south for trial and execution." Oskar paused and looked at Pendal as he said the word "execution" to try and gauge her reaction, which was very limited and told him there may be a bloodline connection, but not an emotional one.

"Those two" Oskar pointed at the fake on and daughter now standing by the horse drawn carriage as the Empress was placed aboard, "they managed to kill the Imperial agents and take back the Empress. They were able to send word she would be on the same transport as you. It was partly good fortune and if she woke I thought a friendly face if she wakes would be good for her." Oskar paused, "I had not thought the Imperials would change strategy and try to assassinate her." He pointed at the three covered bodies and the baby Vanmor. "These agents each have a different way of killing as you discovered."

"Well" said Pendal with a relieved sigh, "it worked out well in the end."

Oskar sucked air through his teeth and looked at her with an oddly energized expression on his face. "The vocal cords of the baby Vanmor had been cut, that is why it did not make any sound. If the eyes are covered and its limbs contained and restricted, it is very docile at that age. When it was thrown at you, the intention was it would bite and claw at you causing a great loss of blood and distracting you. Surviving such an attack would leave you infected with violent disease. To set it on the Empress it would have killed her. The boy with the breath tube, he was the one that would have killed you, or the Empress, all his writing instruments contained poisoned darts. The man, he was just had a blade carrier, nothing special about him."

Oskar and Pendal looked up as the carriage with the Empress left under extremely heavy guard.

"There is more, isn't there?" asked Pendal.

Oskar looked at the astuteness of Pendal's observation. "Do an old man a favour and tell an old friend what you think."

"I would not…" started Pendal but Oskar glared at her, he wanted her thoughts and answers, not a something that would make him feel well. Pendal cleared her throat and looked over at the covered bodies and the baby Vanmor. "I see direction and purpose from someone who is following orders but can improvise, plan and act."

Oskar looked at the covered bodies and then back at Pendal, "How so?" he asked, but, continue."

"The person directing this was successful at intercepting the Empress and killed the guards you sent to protect her, they managed to drug her. But who did this was not able to keep control of the Empress. Your two agents got her back and started to transport her," Pendal indicated the fake son and daughter.

Oskar nodded, "carry on, there is nothing I disagree with so far."

Pendal turned her attention back to Oskar, "your two agents who recovered the Empress got word to you of their achievement and you managed to guide them to the transport I was on. I assume they boarded the transport at the last stop." Pendal looked at Oskar for confirmation, he simply nodded. "By the time they boarded the transport the person directing the Imperial agents changed the plan from taking her south for trial and execution to simple assassination."

Oskar nodded vigorously, his large hairy eyebrows now met in a solid line of concentration.

Pendal continued, "the speed with which a group of three assassins, each with a different killing skill, and a baby Vanmor with no voice was acquired, is perhaps the most disturbing" she said.

Oskar remained silent; he was looking at the small rocks by the side of the transport rails and turning them over with his stick. He stopped and looked over at the covered bodies again and sucked air violently through his teeth.

He turned back to Pendal. "You are the unknown in all of this. Only myself, and those two "guards" I set to follow you knew you were on the transport. But they do not know who you are. They still think of you as a Blade Smith. You must not reveal your bloodline to anyone on any account." With his stick he beat a large rock that lay helpless amongst the small ones, "you are a Blade Smith in everyway Pendal, and your mind is sharp and focused like the fine edge on your blades." He looked down at the tare in her robe on the forearm and the scratch in the armour from the baby Vanmor's claws. "You need new robes and the armour will be replaced."

Oskar started to walk down the slope to the carriage he and Pendal were to continue their journey in. "I can stitch the robes and the armour in only scratched," said Pendal.

Oskar stopped and looked over his shoulder at Pendal, "your armour is excellent but it will be replaced with some that is exquisite in its effectiveness. As for repairing your robe, yes, you could, but we have to prepare for what we want to do next, and plan alternatives if the Imperials try again. And besides, you have blades to sharpen and take care of." The old man returned to look at the carriage waiting for them and continued down the slope with Pendal following.

Pendal leaned against a side table listening to the debate. In her hand she had one of the most simple and tasty things she had encountered since coming north. Cone shaped seeds roasted gently until they split open, when they opened the succulent meat inside was ready to eat. A couple of more steps added very fine ground salt and sometimes spices to the meat. So far Pendal had tasted them without ground salt, spices, ground salt and spices and mixed with a variety of other seeds. Allowed to cool, the seeds were then sold in simple bags almost everywhere. Oskar had explained the seeds were in season, but if carefully preserved after roasting they could be eaten year round.

Pendal breathed deeply and then stood up right, throwing the last of the empty seed shells in the waste cask beside the table. Two officers looked around at the sound of the shells hitting the side of the cask.

"I have never heard so many powerful and influential officers struggle so hard to achieve nothing," said Pendal to the assembled group.

Oskar had been sitting slightly away from the table and the group of officers had it surrounded, his hands folded on the handgrip of his stick and his chin resting on his hands. He looked to be asleep but as Pendal spoke a heavy eyebrow twitched up and the eye under it rotated in her direction. One of his hands unfurled to cover his mouth at the smile that spread over it at what Pendal had said.

Pendal took a moment as chatter around the table stopped and all turned in her direction. She brushed the last of the shells off her robes and she kicked them toward the waste cask. Oskar had been true to his word; the new body armour she had received was exquisite.

As she stood there in the clean beautifully detailed robes of a priest of the order of 1, she was fully covered with armour, it was light and flexible but she had seen it stop multiple small missiles from several projectile weapons all fired at it at the same time. The only thing Oskar could not persuade her to do was to change her boots, he suggested she wear some a little less heavy, he received a hard stare and he never raised the issue again.

Pendal now carried her two blades openly, Oskar's suggestion that she work with a leather worker to make the belts she had been using to hold her blade sheathes more stable and ensure exact positioning of the blade handles had been a good idea and she had said so when the work was complete.

Silence reigned.

Pendal waved some lighting globes from above the table to where she stood by a large, detailed wall mounted map of VodaKhan. She waved her hands in the direction of the huge map. "From the lands to the south all main transport routes go north to the Capital. I happened to join the transport after I arrived from the west. According to the Transport Guardian the assassins joined the transport one stop before the Empress was boarded with the intention of going to the capital. They were seated in the same carriage as myself and the Empress by accident!" exclaimed Pendal. "They were masquerading as a family and wanted to sit together away from other people." As Pendal turned to the assembled officers, she took a tasty piece of a seed from between her teeth and popped it back into her mouth to chew and swallow. "We have to consider it an assassination attempt of pure opportunity," lectured Pendal. "We also have to believe that Imperial forces are more abundant and more flexible than we thought them to be."

Pendal knew it was a message Oskar would understand but the officers at the table less, so. They had large bodies of troops, some obscenely well armed but like most such military units they take time to organize, deploy and manage and there is still no guarantee they will be able to defend against a woman who appears to be carrying a sleeping baby or a young student carrying a tube for his papers, pens and is incessantly chewing.

Pendal's thoughts had not changed, "I am also suggesting we draw out the enemy by using false targets, let them attack those so we have an opportunity to capture and or kill them."

Oskar looked at Pendal intently, "so you see this as an opportunity to draw out Imperial spies and in so doing make VodaKhan stronger?" he asked.

Pendal nodded. She had not thought of making VodaKhan stronger, from all that Lovan had said they were strong enough, all she could think of was making sure there was clarity about what was happening and bringing life back to what it should be and no pretense. Perhaps it was her Garfan upbringing, but she adored simplicity.

Oskar slowly raised himself from his chair, as he did silence fell like a thick fog in the room. He looked around the table and with his stick, he pointed at three officers in mottled dark green battle uniforms, "you with Pendal," he looked at six more, "as happened on the transport, dress someone as an old woman who is under medication and being helped by a son and daughter. Protective guards dressed as ordinary travelers. Start in the south and work your way north to the capital." He paused and looked at Pendal and back at the officers at the table. "We have our own spies who are supposed to be controlling and nullifying Imperial agents, obviously they are not," he paused again and sucked air through his teeth, "maybe we need to refresh them," he said and pointed to the remaining officers.

He looked up at the timekeeper on the wall, "we have been here discussing for four time periods, now is the time to act." The stick he had been using to point to officers at the table he now bright down hard on it which made some of them jump and at least one splashed river liquid from their flask on to themselves and the floor.

As the officers filled out of the room, Pendal moved back to her bag of seeds and scooped a handful to start eating. Oskar waited for her at the door. "You like the simple flavour" it was an observation not a question.

"Yes," replied Pendal, "perhaps it is my upbringing in Garfan, perhaps my guiding spirits appreciate simplicity, this is about bringing back simplicity and simple truths." They left the room together and walked down a short corridor, at the end you could either turn right or left, to the right was a bright light of the outside Day Rise streaming in through a glass door. To the left on both sides of the corridor six heavily armed men stood guard. A single door at the end was almost completely covered by more heavily armed men standing shoulder to shoulder.

Like the liquid of the Great Salt Sea being parted by the ship Pendal had sailed on to the other side, the men parted as she went ahead of Oskar. She opened the door.

Two nurses and two healers stood to attention as she entered the room. The old woman who was so incapable on the train was sitting propped up by cushions with a bowl of mildly spiced herbs for energy and clear thought in her hands, a flask of more liquid was heating on a warmer. Oskar held the door wide for the healers and nurses to leave, as the leading healer passed Oskar, he asked them all to remain outside, he and Pendal would not be long with their patient.

After the door closed, Pendal walked over and hugged the woman, "I am glad you are alright mother," she said.

"Oskar tells me I have you to thank for still being here," she replied and hugged Pendal as best as she was able. "I'm sorry, I cannot hug you better, but what they gave me to sleep is taking a while to get out of this old body."

Pendal took one of the chairs a healer had been siting on close to Lenvar's make shift bed. "Do you remember anything about what happened?" asked Pendal.

Lenvar, looked at the bowl and sipped from it, "I was travelling with two agents, one Imperial that I trusted and one VodaKhan, we had crossed over the Great Valley that acts as part of the southern boundary. We were taking an out of the way route to the Capital and were safe until we joined the main route north. We stopped at different stations on the way north to change horses, eat and take a short rest from riding. I cannot ride like I used to." She looked at Pendal who had started eating her delicious seeds again, and then at Oskar. "In the last station there was more than the usual number of horses and riders, there just seemed to be a lot of people. The last things I remember was a heavy cloth being forced over my face from someone not very tall behind me having difficulty holding it there but the smell of sleeping herbs was very strong. As my eyes started to sleep, I saw the agents I was travelling with being killed."

Pendal slowly chewed at a seed she had just put in her mouth, "do you remember any names, anything said?" She asked.

Lenvar looked back and forth between Oskar and Pendal. "At the stop before the one we were attacked at, I heard someone behind me say, "Callar, must be told!"

"Callar" said Pendal slowly as she added a seed to those still in her mouth, "Callar" she repeated the name again.

Lenvar looked at Pendal and reached out slowly to stroke Pendal's cheek with the back of her hand if she was trying to brush the confusion from Pendal's face. It was a gentle action of a mother trying to smooth away the worries of her child.

"Callar" repeated Pendal, Oskar moved to her side and looked at Lenvar.

"Are you sure that was the name?"

Lenvar nodded slowly, "I heard it spoken three times it was spoken by someone behind me. Then I heard a door open and close, I assumed the speaker of the name left. I did not see them."

Pendal stared at the large wall map of VodaKhan with Oskar and the three officers who had been assigned to her. She continued eating her favourite seeds. The map showed it was possible to ride from the stopping place where Lenvar heard unknown people speak of Callar to the one where she was drugged and taken prisoner by back country roads.

"There is no alternative we must travel that main route north and question and search for Callar," said Oskar. "We need to catch him, alive!"

"And keep him alive" added Pendal. "But it troubles me" she said. "Even if you could ride from the stop where the name was mentioned to the place where the attack took place, there is no time for a message to go to Callar, organize the attack and for the attack to be carried out." Pendal looked at Oskar and then the officers. "The name was spoken three times, if there were three people on the room, then one person could go to tell Callar, and the other two could ride hard to the next stop and commit the attack…." Pendal's voice trailed off but a moment later she continued, "… at the next stop Lenvar said she saw both agents being killed as she was being drugged. That would mean more than two people involved in the attack."

Oskar had brought one of the meeting chairs from the table and was sitting just to the right of Pendal. He made a familiar sucking sound through his teeth, "that is the main route north from the border, if you were an Imperial that would be the fastest way north and there are the most cross routes east and west and back routes to disappear on in that region. Who is the protector for this section?" He looked at the three officers, but he knew he would not receive and answer. None of them were from this region let alone the detailed section they were considering. He rapped the floor hard with his stick. Suddenly, like a child surprised by its parents with a gift, one of the officers looked at Pendal and

Oskar and bolted from the room allowing the door to slam behind him. The other two looked at each other with blank expressions.

"When Oskar asks a question, and you don't know the answer, the best thing to do is go and find it," said Pendal quietly to the two officers.

One season at the Monastery Pendal had been assigned to work in the far plantings. She had ridden horses then, they were big, slow, and built for pulling the carts that brought field plantings back for processing. There were no saddles and the carts had no seats so Pendal and the others in charge of the horses and carts had to ride bareback on the animals with short reins to control them. So unlike the animal she sat on now. This was a well-fed, well-exercised and a very powerful animal bred for speed and endurance. The reigns were not as short as at the monastery and there was a saddle.

Before starting to ride the animal she had taken time to communicate and learn the animals spirit and connect with it. Its spirit was joyful and playful, it was also serious and dedicated, and it enjoyed the life it had, especially when racing hard with other horses. It did not always like having a rider on its back or the saddle, which Pendal adjusted, and the spirit thanked her for the small change that meant so much.

Now Pendal looked down from a hill ridge with trees and thick growing bushes that concealed them. She had special seeing glasses that made it appear she was just a short distance from the buildings where the attack took place, she could see in close detail the people going about their business, taking River Liquid in bowls, food and relaxing from their journey while their horses were attended to.

She chewed and sucked the juice from the leaf of a bush she had picked as they moved in to position. Only one of the officers followed her example and took and chewed the leaf though his face registered his unhappiness at the bitter taste of the juice. Pendal however after years of eating herbs and other plants raw found the taste familiar and cleansing in her mouth.

She felt a nudge from the horse and sensed it wanted her to look to her right. She scanned the hill above and to the right of the buildings, nothing. The horse nudged her again and Pendal looked higher. Yes! She saw it, a grouping of bushes that did not seem quite natural and in amongst them two men, also with the special seeing glasses and projectile weapons. She thanked the strong spirit next to her and received a small playful nudge from the horse in response.

Pendal turned to look at the three elite VodaKhan officers behind her. They too had the special seeing glasses and like Pendal had been looking at the buildings and watching the coming and going of travelers, and servers but seemed to think that was all there was and had put their glasses down. They did no wear their uniforms or have any indication of their military connection and were now adjusting their disguises, Pendal pointed on the hill, the officers picked up their glasses and looked where she pointed and then vigorously nodded that they had found the two men and their hiding place. Then one of the soldiers pointed further along the hill down closer to the main route another two hiding among some rocks.

Pendal sat between the three officers looking down at what appeared to be two servers from the kitchens except they sat with food, river liquid and projectile weapons. The distance between the two groups of lookouts was poorly organized. They were out of sight of each other, and these two did not have any signaling devices.

The two lookouts beneath them were hiding amongst some large rocks, they were truly crammed into the space they had. It was looking down on them that Pendal remembered jumping of a ledge into the River Ohm and swimming in the cool clear liquid. She had spotted a similar ledge above the lookouts. Brushing aside the soldiers she carefully worked her way down to the ledge, as with the ledge she and Vella jumped from, there was only one way to get off the ledge.

Pendal stretched her arms out until they were level with her shoulders, she looked ahead, and she looked down, and then she stepped off.

She landed with her left foot on the back of one mans neck and the other in the middle of his back. She chose him because he was a little heaver and well fed than the other, so Pendal reasoned, the landing might be a bit softer. As her feet met the kitchen server, they flexed violently to help break her fall. The kitchen server was dead with seconds of Pendal landing on him.

The second server was within her blades reach and stared at her in utter uncontrolled amazement and fear. In one scything move, Pendal took her front blade from its sheath and slashed it across his throat. He too was dead before he body hit the boulder behind him. Pendal stepped off the server she had landed on and stood up. She looked up at the officers who were trying to find their way down to the hiding spot without engaging in the leap that Pendal had just executed.

The first to join her in the hideout simply looked up at the ledge and at Pendal with admiration. Then he turned the first body over and started to search the man's pockets. As the other two-joined Pendal and the first officer, the space became crowded so Pendal sat up on a flat bounder as the three went to work.

After the search was complete, which included the dead men's boots, Pendal joined the three soldiers. A mix of papers, some receipts and a few bills for food and liquid that had not been marked off by the cash manager. Both of the servers had timetables for major transports and carriages headed both North and South that provided regular travel service along the route. There was a map that one of the soldiers was comparing to a pocket version of standard issue for VodaKhan soldiers.

Both servers had a fair number of disks on them; they were evidently well-tipped and made plentiful money from travellers. The disks were thrown on the ground but as Pendal stepped back to think a voice, one of her guiding spirits insisted she look at the dirt floor, at the disks. The disks had been thrown to the floor in two piles, one for each server. She bent down and started flipping the coins over but she didn't have to flip all of them; each server had a disk that had holes beaten in to it. Seeing Pendal absorbed by the disks, the others stopped what they were doing and jostled each other to see what she was looking at.

One of the solders took a disk to examine it. Pendal felt his spirits excitement he had an idea what the disks meant.

He took the map the second server had been carrying and by indicating the value of the disk he matched it to the designated route number of one heavily used for moving north from the border. Moving the holes punched in the disk with route stops he was able to identify a location where, as here, there existed a route stop with efficient locations to raid or control carriages and transports. The other disk was a different value, it was easy to match it to the route number they were on, he located the stop where the attack against the empress occurred and it show the spot they stood on was the first of three, not two such vantage points near the route stop.

They studied the map and the location of the other look out they knew of, and the one indicated but they had not found. The risk of being detected was too great. Pendal folded the map around placed the disk and in a pocket, she would ride into the route stop with the three soldiers, following one-by-one.

"A priest!"

Pendal had just dismounted and was stroking the muzzle of her horse and waiting for a horse tender to take him and provide river liquid and grain plantings to him, though the horse gave her every indication he required neither.

In this part of the country, Pendal did not require a heavy cloak to protect her from Day Rise, instead she wore a light jacked that covered her back blade, giving the impression all she had was the blade at her front. The rest of her attire was pure Garfan order maroon, light blue and gold. Oskar's tailors had done a marvelous job of updating and restyling the attire so that it was more attractive, better fitting and covered her body armour perfectly.

The traveller who called out her arrival was urinating at the side of the route stop and found it amusing to be doing that while announcing her arrival. He was a large bald man, rather neatly dressed but appeared to have been travelling for some time as he was unshaven and had been so for several Day Risings.

He threw back his head looking to the beautiful blue sky that could be seen in small patches through the dense trees. As he did a large arc of urine twinkled attractively in the light coming through the trees before landing on the herb plantings.

He filled his lungs as he straightened his clothes and bellowed the words at the top of his voice. "A priest!"

Pendal waited for a server to take her to a table. One of the disguised VodaKhan solders had arrived, as they had agreed, they made no indication they knew each other.

A small server hurried in Pendal's direction, as did the traveller. She could see the traveller was intoxicated, perhaps not significantly but his walk, his demeanor, all pointed to him enjoying the fortified river liquid she saw several others enjoying. At some point, she could see the server and the traveller would collide and indeed they did with the server being knocked into a vacant table and falling to the ground. The traveller feigned an apology at knocking the server down and started to help him up.

Pendal waited.

The traveller's help was part of a game he was playing as the server made it part way to a standing position the traveller would do something that caused the server to fall back down, perhaps use a heavy foot to pull the servers leg away or push the table the server was holding on to so that he lost balance again. This happened three times, finally the traveller allowed the server to stand, but he was not finished, he pushed the server backwards. The server stumbled against a chair, lost his balance, and fell down again.

From inside the stop, Pendal noticed another server and a tall man in the shadows she could not quiet see watching what was happening. The server started to move forward but the man in the shadows held him back.

The traveller now turned his attention to Pendal.

Standing a couple of paces in front of Pendal she could smell the fortified liquid on his breath and see food stains on his shirt. He had bad teeth. The second officer had arrived.

"Does everyone not see this?" he shouted over his shoulder to the other travellers and servers. "We have a priest that needs a table!" He roared at the top of his voice. "A very, very pretty priest." He eyed Pendal from head to toe as if he were deciding what to do next. "I have a sister!" he exclaimed in what he thought was normal speech but it was still quite loud. " I have a sister who is a priest! Yes I do! I don't know what order she is in and I don't care. When our parents died I could not afford to feed my little sister so I took her to the local monastery and they took her in. She cried and kicked and screamed." He stopped talking and whipped away imaginary tears, as he did he shuffled a coupe of half steps towards Pendal.

"Bloody Priest!" he roared and took a wild swing with his right fist at Pendal. It was a slow ponderous swing and Pendal was easily able to flex at the knees and allow the big fist to pass over her head. As she flexed at the knees she took a step to the left and slightly towards the man. She stood up and at the same time brought her right arm across her body and swung her elbow into the man's ribs just below his armpit. There was the distinctive crack of a rib breaking and the man screamed in pain. He started to swing around to punch Pendal with his other fist.

While his moves were slow and ponderous, hers were tight, elegant, coordinated and swift. Pendal dodged the second fist easily by flexing and ducking again at the knees; she brought both fists up together, tightly aligned in a double punch connecting with the man's jaw. The power and elegance of the double punch sent him backwards against a table, which he rolled off on to the dirt floor. He was unconscious before he hit the floor. The third officer arrived.

She heard a voice in her head, "Look on the Hill!" One of Pendal's guardian spirits was talking to her, she turned and looked up the hill behind the stop, as she did one of the officers came over to ask, as a good fellow rider on the route would if she were alright. He followed Pendal's gaze.

Almost at the top of the hill, they could see a server taking the final steps to the top and then pass over the crest. They briefly looked at each other as the Pendal audibly thanked him for his help but assured him she was OK. They both knew that time was counting, either the server was going to get help or he was going to check on the other lookouts. As soon as he found the furthest ones dead, the alarm would be raised.

Pendal moved a table close by the door of the inner serving area, which looked dark, dusty and reminded her of a childhood story told by the priests at the monastery. The story said that all the good things they saw around them came from great mines where the bad, evil and non-believers were forced like slaves to hew them. The story went on to say that if the supplicants did not do what they were told when they were outside the monastery walls, such as when they were harvesting river creatures for the kitchens or like Pendal, out under Moon Rise tending the plantings, they could fall or be led into one of the mines from which they would return only after they had lived and slaved there for many, many lives. When or if they were finally allowed back to the surface, the first body their soul inhabited would be broken and painful.

The story frightened the young Pendal and all the other supplicants of her age and was told over and over until one evening out in the plantings when she had squatted by the cart and her first period flowed. All three moons had been in the sky and the air had been cool and crisp, the tenth third period of the cycle was about to start, the plantings were already starting to grow smaller and some were already drawing back into the ground soil to prepare for the cold of the last period of the year. But for Pendal the flow from her body was magical. The magic took away the fears and worries she had grown up with through the early years. It was the ending of a part of her life and she was moving to the next.

As she looked at the dark, smoky inner seating area it did not scare her, but it was also somewhere she did not need to go if she did not have to. There was a table where the sun filtered through on to it and she could sit with her back to a stout wall preventing anyone getting behind her.

Her server was a young boy. Short light brown hair and yellow liquid eyes, a small scar split is top lip and she could see he was missing the tip of one of his fingers on his right hand. His shirt was clean and dirty all at the same time. He was barefoot. Pendal was not sure about his age, only that the belt on his pants was about the height of the table.

"What does the priest want?" He spoke quietly, slowly, and with care when forming his words but perhaps not caring what the words were thought Pendal, but then she thought, he only knows what I am from my clothing.

"Clean river liquid and…" she thought for a moment, she did not feel hungry. She named a simple root preparation but asked for extra spices to be provided which she would add herself.

Around the open eating area, the three officers had tables and were ordering. As agreed, they would order simple things and be careful with eating, they did not want to be drugged by sleeping herbs as the Empress had, though in her case the herbs had been provided on a cloth over her face.

Pendal took three deep breaths and sat back against the wall. It was nice here. She looked up at the bright green colours of the tree leaves and the Day Rise brightness filtering through and for the first time since sitting on the hill on the fare side of The Great Salt Sea she entered the mantra of giving up her worries and cares to her guiding spirits and all the others who watched over her.

Pendal took three more deep breaths and mentally drew the symbol that would seal the gift of her cares to the spirits.

As she brought her focus down to the eating area, she could see one of the officers being served and one already eating.

"Food for the priest and clean river liquid!" The boy had already returned and was setting out a bowl of liquid and several bowls of spices and her root dish. The boy held his serving tray to his chest as if hugging it and named the cost of the meal. Pendal pulled out a couple of disks from her pouch plus one of the two disks with the holes punched in it.

The Boy calculated the difference between the cost of the meal and what Pendal was giving him and bowed to her. "Is the difference my benefit, if so it is a lot." He said.

A word of inspiration from one of her guides appeared in her mind, Pendal looked at the boy and turned her reply from a simple yes into a blessing. "This priest provides benefit to you so you may live and grow to be a true believer. Let no one take it away." The boy smiled and placed his hands in tight fists and pressed them together in front of him and bowed as if in prayer and then turned and left to take the disks to the Cash Register.

Pendal's stare followed the boy. Just inside the dark mouth of the interior sat the Cash Register. An old man sitting at a small table, there was a writing instrument on the table plus paper on which he registered the meals, their cost, the server and the amount paid, he recorded the benefit if any awarded to the server for good service. From the benefit, he deducted costs and paid the server the remainder. He had one eye.

The boy handed the disks to the Cash Register who looked at the cost of her meal and held the disks in his hand as he counted the value Pendal had paid. The boy waited patiently. The Cash Register looked up at Pendal in surprise when he realized the difference. Then he wrote on the paper and started to count the boy's benefit from piles of disks that Pendal could see from their colour would give the boy very little.

Slowly with her left hand she picked up a bowl and emptied it on the floor and then slammed it on her table. The sharp sound resounded around the eating area but attracted little attention from the other diners, not even the officers who were with her. But the Cash Register looked up and at Pendal.

Pendal made an almost universal sign of a knife, cutting something, but she did it under her right eye, it happened that his only remaining eye was his right. They stared at each other for several moments. Pendal repeated the hand sign under her right eye and then pointed at him. Then she held up three fingers. The message was clear; if he did not provide the correct benefit to the boy he would lose his other eye. He opened his mouth to reveal yellow broken teeth and he scowled back at Pendal. Pendal folded one finger away, the Cash Register spat a ball of brown mucus on the ground, the boy nervously looked over at Pendal and tried to signal to her that she must not do anything to make the Cash Register angry. Pendal, still staring at the man again pointed at her right eye and then at the Cash Register. There was only one finger raised now.

As Pendal started to lower her finger the Cash Register took seven disks from a pile closer to his side of the table. And set them one by one on the table. Pendal shook her head and with her hand indicated he must move back. It was something she learned early at the monastery, even if something is due to you, and it is agreed, sometimes the giver will extract a price from you. At the monastery, it was candles to light their room. The Priests would set out on a table the candles each supplicant was entitled to, much like the Cash Register had done with the disks. As the supplicant reached for each candle the priest would beat the hand with a hardened piece of root vine. The number of candles the supplicant took away from the table was a sign of the amount of pain they could endure.

Pendal had always been able to endure a lot of pain and often came away with all of her entitlement of candles but with her hands bruised and bloodied.

Again there was a stand off, Pendal held up three fingers. At two fingers, the old man turned his face slightly to one side and held his nose with two fingers and snorted on to the floor. Pendal looked past the Cash Register and could just make out someone at a table a little further in the dark space, watching. As the trees waved in the wind and allowed more Day Rise Light to filter through she could catch a glimpse of hands and a long straight nose and a wide mouth. There was now one finger held up. From on his lap the old man brought out a stick about length of his forearm, as he did this, the boy backed away from the table placing benefit he was entitled to out of reach.

Pendal took out her front blade and used its incredibly sharp edge to carve off a piece of the table the length if her hand. She sheathed the blade and held up the sizable piece of wood she had removed.

The old man put the stick down on his lap and backed away from the table. The boy was so fast at moving to the table to collect his benefit that he jostled the table. The boy backed away with his benefit clasped in his hand, and then he turned around to walk away and stash his benefit, as he did, he looked at Pendal with a broad smile.

Pendal returned to look at her table and examine the bowls and the food. The river liquid was in a clear glass bowl, the liquid was so clear that until the bowl was moved the bowl did not appear to contain anything. The other food bowls were also of glass. Pendal turned each of the bowls so that the spot facing her was facing away from where she would place her mouth.

Pendal looked up to see the third officer being served, and she closed her eyes. The officer had been served bowls that were dark ceramic and he had started using the bowls as they had been set out for him. He had not as Pendal had done rotated the bowls and he had ordered food that required placing eating implements in his mouth.

At the monastery Pendal had worked for a time in the small hospital that provided care and healing to all in the order and sick travelers were admitted for care. Some, especially travelers who feared being drugged and robbed, would not take their herbs and other medicines even though it would heal them. In those cases, the medicines were prepared in such a way that they were tasteless. When Pendal administered to someone refusing to take their medications she would smear it on her fingers and thumbs and when handling the meal bowls she would place her fingers and thumbs where the patients mouth would go and leave a smear of medication behind.

Spreading medications on eating implements the patient would put in their mouth was the easiest way of all to get a larger amount of medicine into the patient. They never tampered with the food so that the patient was less likely to detect what was happening. However, dark ceramic bowls and similar food containers had to be used to make sure the smeared coatings could not be seen.

The clear glass as she had been presented with was one of the best ways to detect if anything had been placed on the bowl's surface, rotating it so the place on the bowl presented was away form where the mouth went added a little extra protection.

The other two officers Pendal could see had similar food to the first but the one who chewed the leaves had something simpler and without eating implements. He nodded slightly at Pendal, he had been watching and agreed the boy should take all the benefit Pendal intended him to have.

Nevertheless, Pendal noted a very slight off colour swirl in one of the dry spice bowls. She pushed it aside.

She ate small amounts of the food and drink minimal amounts of the water, yet her actions with the bowls were elaborate and anyone watching would assume she was eating heartily.

As she set her bowl of river liquid down she looked around, the dinning area. There were less people eating, several transport carriages had rolled through, one headed south, two north. None of them had off loaded passengers, all had taken on people who were well fed and would probably sleep for a period or so of their journey. There were no travellers, as Pendal appeared to be, alone, and the person she had punched unconscious had recovered and left on a northbound transport.

The officer who had ordered and eaten without any sort of precautions was sleeping peacefully sprawled across his table; several food bowls had been knocked on the floor when he passed out. The second officer was looking drowsy but appeared to be awake. Whether he would be any use in a fight Pendal had no idea of knowing and did not count on him. There was one remaining officer who looked fully awake but bored and probably too full with his meal.

The server she had seen disappearing over the hill behind the route stop had returned ashen faced and had gone directly inside to the table that had been watching the stand off with the Cash Register. The server had delivered what he wanted to say and then been sent away by the person hidden in the darkness.

While the person at that dark inner table was thinking, Pendal stood momentarily to ensure her she had unrestricted access to both her blades. She also adjusted the body armour, which Oskar had promised she would not know she was wearing, and indeed, she did not. She signaled to the remaining officer on whom she believed she could call to action and ne nodded he was ready.

"Priest!" it was an exclamation not a word that was spoken. The voice was clean and crisp. "Was the meal good?" asked the man in front of her table. He had appeared shortly after Pendal had reseated herself. "Are the spices sufficient on a beautiful Day Rise like today?" he asked.

Pendal had prepared herself for meeting her dead brother Callar and when she looked at the speaker, she gave not the slightest indication of recognition but the similarities between the man standing there and Lovan, the NighT Guardian, and Cavahn were unmistakable. He was tall like Cavahn but unlike Lovan he did not have the musculature of his father the NighT Guardian. He had the same thick long hair of his mother and Lovan but it appeared even darker. He had the same liquid red eyes of Cavahn and Lovan.

Pendal looked at his steps left on the dirt floor and could see a shift of weight from left to right; it was probable that one leg was slightly shorter than the other, useful to know in a fight.

Without asking, he pulled out the chair opposite Pendal and sat down. He leaned forward, placing his elbows at the edge of the table and interlaced his fingers, and then he leaned a little further forward so that his first fingers were just under his nose and his mouth was covered.

"Which order?" The question was blunt and did not follow his other words.

"The meal was good," and the "…spices were sufficient for any Day Rise, beautiful or not," replied Pendal and paused, "Garfan!" she exclaimed. She preferred not to say she was a priest of the order of 1, the same as Cavahn.

There was a pause in the conversation as he took in her answers.

Pendal was aware of the word and mind game he had clearly thought he would play on her.

The Priests at the monastery played it almost daily on any supplicant they felt like. They would ask disjointed questions and questions they did not require an answer in rapid succession with questions they did want an answer to. Sometimes the important or valuable questions were ones that should be evaded or simply not answered. The supplicant often did not know whether the answer to a questions was valuable or not, or should be answered or not amongst a torrent words. In the monastery, the questions that mattered had to do with the order, a mix of secrets the order wanted kept secret and some intentions and motives that could not be allowed to escape the walls.

To answer a question incorrectly earned the supplicant a beating.

He looked at her, no, he stared at her, "I cannot win," he said.

Pendal did not answer, she had returned his gaze and would answer on her terms in her time. "You have not begun to lose," she said "but loss is certain with your current approach" she finished.

He continued to stare at her but eventually he slowly sat back in his chair, taking his elbows from the table and allowing Pendal to see his full face. His chin was rounded and his mouth, small and tight.

"Priest, you are a very, very long way from the Garfan monastery." Now he sat back and looked at her as if the extra distance allowed him to judge the reply as its sounds came across the greater space between them.

"I will go as far as my mission to bring light, love, and friendship to this world needs me to go," replied Pendal.

"So, you will not stop here?" he asked.

"I will not!" said Pendal firmly.

Although he was trying to be conversational in is tone and approach now, Pendal continued with the direction and firmness, she had learned in prayer in the small chapel she and a few others had been allowed to pray in. Reverence for the Holy Spirit that cared for all creatures and to which their souls spoke was free of elaboration, superfluous words. Even the tone of the supplicants voice was stripped of any indication of happiness and sadness in that chapel.

Pendal had years of training in how to behave and respond in the war of words being fought now across the table. He had so much less and for the first time she understood what Vella meant back on the verandah when she had told Pendal that there are people who study and take the oath and who are then are trained to be members of the directorate. Pendal, Vella had said, had lived the oath every day of her existence in the Garfan order.

Pendal felt immensely strong at that moment, not arrogant, not overly confident, she was "solid," as they would say at the monastery. Things and people that were believable were solid like the stone of the walls or the buildings and she masked it skillfully, another talent she had learned in the order.

"What will happen next?" he asked.

"What happens depends on you Callar," she replied. As she said the words she sat back against the chair to give her hands maximum freedom to reach her blades and she moved her feet apart so as to give herself better freedom of movement.

She looked over at the remaining officer who was not unconscious; two new people were sitting at a table behind him. She gave a small hand signal prepare to leave. As he did he saw the two people seated behind him and as she expected and wanted, he became defensive.

The man sitting opposite Pendal stared at her with deep concentration. The fact she knew his name did not register alarm or concern, "Since when does a priest care who I am or what I am doing?" he asked.

"This priest as I told you is here to bring peace and loving light, to do that I work against dark and lower energies," she said. As she said these words, she hand signed to the remaining officer that they had their prey, he turned and left, heading for the horse yard where their rides were resting.

"So, I am a dark or lower energy?" he asked. "And yes, my name is Callar," he said.

"That is good to know, I will tell our family when I next see them," she replied, and paused. "No you are not a dark or lower energy but your clear clean soul is being used by someone who is." She said.

"I am glad I am not a dark or lower energy, all I do I do for the betterment of the people here and in the lower regions," he said. Then he stiffened in his seat, "What do you mean, our family," he asked.

Pendal casually looked away to her right and saw the officer mount his horse and leave hers tied at the front of the horse yard, when she needed her horse, she would not have to go searching for it. She did not reply to the question from Callar about family. She let the unanswered question burn in his curiosity and distract him. She looked back at Callar for a moment and pointed to the bowls, "which one?" she asked. She spoke over Callar's words, ignoring him and his questions about "our family."

Pendal glanced along a road running west, not north or south from the route stop and saw the officer take out his signal mirror and flash a signal, first to someone she could not see and then to her, as agreed. Pendal stood, moving away from the table and the confused Callar. She started to walk towards her horse.

"You cannot say something like that and then leave!" he exclaimed.

"I can and I will," replied Pendal. "As a priest, I cannot lie, you are aware of that" she stood and turned but did not present her back to Callar. Instead she walked slightly sideways, always keeping him in clear sight. She was now at the edge of the route, Callar placed a hand on her arm to try and make her stop. Instinctively, as Pendal's turned to face Callar her other hand moved to her back blade, to anyone else, it looked as if she was adjusting her robe, as he did not remove his hand from her arm she placed her hand firmly on the blade's handle.

From across the route, Pendal could sense her ride was aware of his fellow horses approaching, many of them, and very quickly.

In that moment, Callar's mind cleared, he was no longer interested in family and what Pendal had said, and he was looking at her arm. He could feel the body armour under her robe and realized she was much more than a priest. "You are the Blade Smith that killed our assassins on the transport!" he blurted out and jerked his hand away from her to give himself fighting space. As he did, VodaKhan soldiers rounded the corner from both northbound and southbound directions, their horses raging to get to their goal.

Callar had not moved far enough away from Pendal, he remained well within her range of attack. Her feet shuffled quickly on the solid compact ground and she lashed out with her right foot and made contact with Callar's upper right leg.

The bone snapped.

Callar screamed loudly and started to fall, his hands grasping wildly for anything to hold on to stop his fall. Behind Pendal, chairs moved back violently and clattered as they fell over. The two who had sat behind the officer moved to protect Callar but the distance from where they were sitting was too great, and they were too slow.

Pendal kicked at Callar's hand as he reached for his blade. She caught the hand side on, breaking several bones in it and making it impossible for him to form a grip on the blades handle. The bigger of the two guards came within blade distance of Pendal. She swirled around on her heel and for a moment she was like a spinning top given to supplicants at the monastery. The tops were decorated with the Order's colours and spun freely in games where the winner made their top spin the longest.

As she spun her back blade came out held by the iron grip Pendal gave it. The blade slashed across the guard's hand and the tendons in it, his blade started to fall out as he could no longer grip it and he opened his mouth to scream in pain. Still spinning Pendal's armour covered elbow came swinging across and struck him under the nose and on his upper row of teeth. He reeled backwards in to the other guard, knocking that one off balance. As the bigger guard continued to fall away from Pendal blood and teeth splattered on to the ground from.

Pendal used her continued spinning momentum to throw her away from the writhing Callar and the struggling guards. As she came to a stop in the middle of the route, VodaKhan guards saturated the dinning area. The officer who had sent the signal rushed in to provide direction, before he could get too far away from her, Pendal screamed at him and pointed in the direction of the Cash Register who was struggling to get out of his chair and had knocked over his table with a wealth of disks on it. The officer directed four soldiers to apprehend him.

Pendal turned to hear the heavy plodding sound of a horse intended to carry great weight come to a stop and shouting, as Oskar demanded help dismounting from the animal. But help was disorganized and insufficient. Pendal walked over looking at Oskar as he waved his stick in the air trying to give direction to officers and men that already knew what to do.

She stood in front of the animal and scratched its nose. She pressed her forehead to the animal's forehead and connected with the animals' spirit. It was an older spirit that had spent many years in the service of the VodaKhan army pulling carts full of provisions and men. It would spend part of its summer in fields rich with plantings it could eat and he the gentle horse it wanted to be.

Pendal scratched around its ears and asked it to kneel so that rider could slide off its back. Without a thought the animal slowly got into a kneeling position and Oskar slid off landing slightly unsteadily but did not fall. As Pendal played with the animal's ears, it slowly got to its feet. She turned to a handler waiting now to take the horses reigns. "You will take this wonderful spirit over to beside the one I am using and make sure," she held her fist at the handler, "he is to be fed and given liquid, and that he is not scared. Do you understand?"

The handler gingerly took the reigns and bowed to Pendal and said he did.

Oskar looked at Pendal a complete look of surprise and a little respect, "You talk to animals?" he asked.

Pendal laughed, "All animals have a guiding spirit, like ours it has needs and wants that should be satisfied. And, if asked, it will help us. I could not think of any other way to get your feet on the ground."

As Pendal spoke the unconscious officers were taken past them on make shift carriers made from tabletops. Oskar frowned and was about to speak but Pendal spoke first. "Don't be too hard on them. I will tell you how it is done, I used it often with patients at the monastery hospital," she said.

Oskar turned back to Pendal, "that monastery has taught you many things and given you many unique gifts though I am sure it did not seem like it at the time," he said.

Pendal's deep seat of strength that she felt when Callar had first sat down remerged as she stood there, but now it was vastly more powerful, concentrated, and focused through her spirit.

Oskar came to stand by her and watch his men restrain and prepare for transport the Cash Register as well as both restrain and treat the still screaming and cursing Callar. Others who had still been at the stop eating and were caught up in the melee and action were being restrained and moved to the transport carriages.

Pendal saw movement in the back of the dark cave mouth of the interior. The boy. The server. She turned to an officer close to her and snapped an order to him that the boy must be retrieved from inside. The officer who was new to being with Pendal and was unaware of her rank at Oskar's right hand; the officer looked at Pendal simply as a priest and did not move, as he started to turn away from her he was struck hard across his back by Oskar's stick, cursed at, and then prodded in the ribs to move quickly to do as she said.

As the soldiers completed their search and loading the prisoners to the transport carriages, the officer returned with two of his mean holding the boy between them. The boy glared fiercely at Pendal and Oskar and tried to spit at Pendal but missed, his mucus ending on the floor several arm lengths away.

"I thought you were a nice," hissed the boy.

Pendal looked the boy directly in the eyes which seemed to alarm the boy, "and I know you are not!" she said.

The questioning of those taken from the route stop had revealed some small and obvious things about the stop itself. It was a place where thieves preyed on people traveling north and south. Pure and simple, pick pockets, and some operating by threatening the travellers to give up money and valuables. The lookouts that Pendal and her officers had identified were part of that activity. They were controlled by the Cash Register at the stop and were to identify targets and like all those involved they were allowed to a keep a percentage of what they stole for their own use.

There had been a signaling system to alert those at the stop that a good target was on the route, or that soldiers were coming but at the time Pendal and the officers were there it was broken. The two they attacked signaled up the route to a man and women who were to signal the two closest to the stop, the robbers at that point would have time to pass the message to their confederates and to the Cash Register who would be prepared for their arrival. When Pendal and the officers were spying out the signaling system, it happened that the man and woman had left to copulate behind the hill.

Pendal stood with her back against the wall, just out of range.

The boy sat at the questioning table. His wrists firmly locked to the table top in front of him, the table, and chair he sat on were solidly locked to the floor. He fidgeted violently in his restraints and aimed alternating curses and spat mucus at Pendal. He reminded her of a wild dog they had caught one Moon Rise eating roots and other nutritious plantings. It was normal for wild animals to raid the plantings and the monastery always grew extra both to make up for what was eaten but as an act of generosity to feed wandering animals of the Great Spirit. But the wild dog they caught had been seen regularly and had become bold and threatened supplicants tending the plantings.

Pendal was waiting.

The boy like the wild dog was too aggressive and violent to be reasoned with, when the dog had become tired and exhausted it accepted it was confined and had lost its freedom and quieted down.

Pendal had tried communicating with the animals spirit to try and diffuse the aggression and quiet it more quickly but she had been too young and the restless spirit she had connected with was too strong and violent and it had scared her, she had sat back and let the restraints do their work. The spirit Pendal sensed in the boy was dark and thrashing, more violent than what she saw physically in the room.

Pendal was a so much, much stronger now and had no doubt she could reach out and diffuse the darkness in the boy and replace it with warm bright, healing light but she held back. She recognized there were times for different approaches and the boy was a person, not a dog, he had to change himself, by himself, using his own mind and the part of his sprit that still remained.

The boy's head rolled back and he let out a great howl of anguish, tears started running down his face and drool from his mouth. He rested his head between his arms locked to the table and sobbed. His shoulders and his back shuddered as he cried. One time he looked up at Pendal and sobbed even louder.

Finally, as with the wild dog, it was over.

Pendal did not move.

"Why did you do it?" she asked.

Still chocked by the convulsions and emotions that had come pouring out, the boy slowly answered, "it was all I was allowed to do."

"Who taught you?" she asked. Pendal thought she knew the answer but wanted to wait to hear it.

"The old man, the Cash Register, he taught me everything." The boy stopped, he sniffled and coughed. "He taught which herbs to pick and how to combine them. He taught me how to administer them by smearing the drugs on my fingers and then on to the bowls. Never poison the food, they may sense it, poison the bowls and implements they use." The boy stopped and his eyes took on a steady stare as he looked across at the wall. "Are you here because of the old lady I gave sleeping drugs to?" He turned to look at Pendal. "That's it, you are here because of her."

Pendal nodded.

"He said he had seen her many years ago when he was young down in the southern regions. He said she was valuable. He said Callar would be very interested in her." The boy coughed again and spat on the floor, near his chair this time, not at Pendal. "He said Callar would take her south and give her to the Emperor as a present and the Emperor would kill her. Then we would all be rich."

"When did Callar arrive?" asked Pendal.

The boy heaved a huge sigh and set his head down on the table again between his locked arms. His reply was almost not heard, "about a Day Rise, maybe a little longer, we sent a fast horse and rider for him."

Pendal turned and left the room.

Oskar was standing outside waiting for her. He had ben watching and listening through a special window that did not reveal itself in the room as it was made to look like part of the wall. "My respect for you continues to grow, we will send the boy to a young person's prison," he said.

"I would rather he go to a monastery of an order that can provide strong direction as well as some love and care, " said Pendal.

Oskar studied her for a long moment and then said he would arrange it, he knew of such a place.

As they walked along the corridor, Oskar disclosed what they had learned from the Cash Register. There was another organized band of robbers and thieves on the other route indicated by the second coin Pendal had retrieved, soldiers were removing them as they talked.

It appeared Callar had fallen in with them because it was convenient and their structure and manpower were already in place. The route he had been captured on was regarded as the main route north and south, all he had to do was wait for "persons of interest" to pass by and then use the robbers to carry out his instructions. They would be rewarded from Imperial money Callar had access to and he promised them greater wealth when the Emperor invaded and took control of VodaKhan.

They turned in to a small office and Oskar closed the door. Pendal moved to the open window. Day Rise was ending; she could see the red glow of its end starting to spread across the sky. Tall trees stood guard outside allowing cool tree scented breezes to came in and give her an intense longing to be out amongst them, walking and connecting with the nature guides that helped the trees and plantings grow in abundance.

Instead she was inside immersed in the deadly tricks and troubles created by human ego.

Oskar joined her at the window and was silent.

"There is more," Oskar said as he broke the beautiful silence. "Callar dispatched a rider south, an Imperial agent no doubt with news of the Empresses' capture. The Cash Register does not know exactly whom Callar told the agent to tell. I would say non less than the Emperor but it is likely it included the route she would be brought to the southern border."

"I was north bound on the transport" said Pendal slowly, her eyes fixed on some bushy tree animals chasing each other around and around a tree. One animal, the one higher up on the tree considered it owned the tree and with it all the nuts and berries it produced, the other was an intruder trying to climb the tree and steal the tree's bounty and was being chased off. Eventually the intruder lost its grip on the tree and fell to the ground, it rolled away in a tight furry ball until it rolled up against another tree. It uncurled itself and groomed itself for a few moments and then scampered up the tree until Pendal lost site of it amongst some branches.

Oskar looked at her quizzically, "I can have all the furry tree creatures you could ever want brought to you," he said.

Pendal sneezed. The air born seeds that floated like dust on the wind had entered the window and she had inhaled them. Just as out in the plantings under moonrise, there were some herbs that sent out their hope for a new generation the same way, and those made her sneeze as well.

"No, leave them there, they are happy," replied Pendal.

"How do you know they are happy," he asked.

"I can sense it, I can connect with their guides, all animals have guides, just as we do." She looked up at the tree and could now see the furry tree creature. It was high up sitting at the point where a branch came out of the tree. It was sitting with its back against the tree and its legs stretched out on the branch. Between its front paws it held a large seed and was peeling it with its sharp front teeth.

"The fastest way south, if you are not taking this route is to head north a short distance and then west, cross the next valley, and then down the route on the far side. You were northbound on that route. Callar's assassins would have been there in very little time. They would have known the schedules of all the transports, north and south bound," he said.

Pendal sighed, "What are we going to do with Callar?"

Oskar did not reply, he was watching another battle on the tree that Pendal had first been watching, the same furry tree creature was trying to stop another climb his tree and steal his seeds and berries, but as he confronted that would be thief, another furry creature, that could just been seen on the side of the tree was climbing unhindered.

"Fascinating aren't they? Asked Pendal smiling.

Oskar turned to look at her and shook himself and tapped the floor with his stick, "Stupid tree creatures!" he exclaimed. Then more slowly and carefully, "he is a spy and he did kidnap a person, regardless of whether she is the Empress and trying to hide from the Emperor. He should be executed. However, he is your half brother." Oskar looked at Pendal for any reaction to the idea Callar should be executed.

"I do not care whether he is my half brother or not, I feel no connection to him, and have no reservation about his fate as a result for his actions," said Pendal in a surprisingly clear and level manner that even surprised her. "The boy said they had to send a rider for Callar, and that it may have taken more than one Day Rise for the Callar to arrive. Where was he?" asked Pendal.

Oskar's eyebrows suddenly rose up. "I had forgotten that, yes, we need to know where he was!" he exclaimed.

Callar was quiet, he was trying to heal as best he could, a broken leg and several bones in his blade hand were also broken. He lay on a sleeping cot staring at the peeling paint on the ceiling. The cot was placed in the room so that he could not see who entered and left and the herbs for the pain were making a little delirious. If all the door openings and closings had been a person coming in or leaving, there would be so many people in the room now that they would have to be standing on him to all fit, he was so, so confused.

The room had no window, only the door.

He did not know whether it was still Day Rise or Moon Rise had begun.

Pendal had brought the chair she was sitting on with her in to the room. The chair and the cot were all furniture in the room.

"So, shall I start or will you?" she asked. There was no response from Callar; his eyes were fixed on the peeling paint on the ceiling. She had been sitting there for some time, trying to connect with Callar's guiding spirit, which seemed as confused as he looked, his memory contained many images, but they were a mixture of chasing ground animals amongst the tall reeds at home when he was below hip height, peaceful nights looking at the second moon which was high in the sky when Cavahn had birthed him and watching the boy servant practice how he administered sleeping herbs to travellers by smearing them on the bowls just as they were served.

In those images the Cash Register swam in and out like some black marauding predator that ate the images and destroyed what he did not like, which was most things.

Pendal had given up trying to connect with Callar's spirit.

Callar closed his eyes, a few moments later his mouth opened. "I was to disrupt and destroy," he said in a peaceful, conversational tone. "The Emperor said I was to disrupt and destroy." Then he fell asleep.

Pendal froze for a moment, trying to understand what had been said. She stood quickly, sending the chair back and over on the floor. She rushed for the door.

"Oskar!" she shouted as she walked back to the room where they had watched furry tree creatures scamper up and down trees, and roll along the ground. He had been at the window watching the little creatures and heard her shout his name. He was half way across the room when she flung the door open. "His mission, given he said by the Emperor, is to disrupt and destroy!" she exclaimed. "What is close by – A Day Rise away that could be involved?" she asked.

Suddenly.

Outside there was chaos.

Soldiers running, horses, struggling with their riders, carts being loaded with supplies, shouting, endless shouting, Oskar held his stick out as a senior officer ran by him in the corridor and stopped him. The man turned to Oskar and without being asked provided the answer to Pendal's question inside, "the great river barrier in the next valley has failed, some say there were loud explosions in the generation house before the failure. There are many, many drowned in the villages that look up to the barrier."

Oskar removed his stick and the officer ran on.

Pendal and Oskar looked down on the devastation from high on the valley wall.

There was destruction and death everywhere, people, farm animals and many, many wild animals. It was on a scale Pendal had never seen before. The generation house where it appeared the explosions had occurred was part of the barrier wall, not separate from it, this made it one of the older barriers in the VodaKhan region Oskar explained. Failure of the generation house had weakened the barrier, which had given way under the pressure of the lake liquid behind it.

The villages and farms that had taken advantage of the rich ground soil when the barrier was built were washed away when the lake liquid came rushing through.

Pendal had sensed death, anguish and pain before, once at the monastery when there had been a fire and several supplicants and farm animals had died. But this was on a scale she had never encountered. What surprised was that she did not sense it when it happened, when these people and animals were dying. All she could think was that her obsession with the world of spies, their webs of deceit and belief that the small things they were doing made big differences, and that the sacrifices the made or caused were worth it. These had blinded her to messages from her guiding spirits and broken her sense of connection with the world around her.

"Pendal…. Pendal!" it was Oskar speaking in a quiet voice. "I have started to understand how you connect with people, animals, and even places. It is a remarkable gift, one you were born with, but the souls that cried out as they were swept away did not cry out to you." He looked at Pendal for some response.

She looked down at the blue and gold ropes that hung from her belt at her left side. She stared at the neat tasseled ends in her hand. "I don't know who or what they cried out to, I didn't sense anything and that brings me pain, Pain of lack of understanding, this is the first time anything on this scale has happened near me and I do not understand why I did not even sense the tiniest ripple of it when it happened," she said.

"If it is any consolation," said Oskar, "Callar could not have done this alone. There are guards and there are workers. It is massively built, there would have been a lot of explosives required to break the generation house away from the wall so that it would collapse." Oskar paused, "we will have to move to the capital now. We have done all we can here. And the senior guardians will want to speak to you and the Dekar-sa Empress. I will do what I can for Callar, but his own words have convicted him."

Pendal looked at Oskar with cold hard eyes. "You had better keep him from me. I am very capable of killing him myself for what has happened here," her voice was hard and brittle. She started to move past Oskar but he stopped her.

"Pendal, if, or when the Emperor is removed from power, you are the next Empress, it is your throne. With your mother behind you and for what you have done here, in

VodaKhan there will be Legions of VodaKhan troops at your back. But the next battles will be fought with your words, your mind, your focus, and your gifts to sense others, not so much with your blades. But always keep those close at hand and sharp!"

Pendal heard the words of wisdom, she knew too well from her life in the order that blades are not the answer to everything. She had had the freedom to fight the physical battles, which she enjoyed, especially since Cavahn and Vella had worked so hard on her mental, and physical training. Now it was time to show that blade sharp focused mind everyone in the order said she had.

Pendal looked at her reflection in the looking glass.

Set in an ornate wooden frame on an equally ornate wooden stand, the looking glass reflected her from head to toe and what she saw far exceeded what the High Priest at the order had seen just before she closed the door on Pendal and left her alone in front of the monastery that night. The gold in the maroon and gold braided rope that hung from her belt was made with real gold, not rope that had been coloured gold. The tassels at the end were made with special rope that was a mix of the maroon coloured gold and normal, yellow gold thread and not one simple colour as was usual. The maroon fabric of her robes and the cloak were soft but strong, she did not know what it was called but it had a beautiful sheen to it that exuded power and conferred that power on the wearer.

The high collar at her neck was decorated with symbols from the order of 1 that affirmed her status as a priest, and something she was not aware of, the Garfan order had conferred the status of Blade Smith on her. It was a rarely given status she did not know existed until she received the honour roll sent by messenger from the High Priest. As part of the honour, the collar was not maroon like the rest of her dress it was as black as the blade she left the monastery with. Underneath she wore her body armour; it was now her second skin to her. A second complete set stood on a body double to one side of the mirror. At her waist front and back were her blades, and her boots had been polished to an impossibly high shine of a maroon and black, which she had not seen before, a throwing blade was in each boot as usual.

She adjusted the collar to better display the symbols and as she did so she started to laugh. It seemed a black collar was the sign of the Blade Smith in VodaKhan as well. The High Protector had introduced her to a black collard VodaKhan Blade Smith, they had chatted easily but Pendal had to say she was ignorant of some of the technical moves he described in great detail. A sparring match had been decided on for the next Day Rise. Her would-be opponent had asked how they would score; apparently there were more ways to score a match than the number of fingers on her hand. Pendal had replied the only way she could, the only way she knew from the monastery, by the opponents blood on the winners blade. At that her opponent's face had gone as white as the glow of Third Moon and other reasons became more pressing uses for the time required for a match.

Her long black hair was almost past her waist now. It had been trimmed and tidied but its length was now managed and controlled by weaving it through a hair catcher made of maroon and gold braided rope.

Her deep maroon red eyes were clear, exceptionally clear. The past several Day Risings had allowed her time to meditate and reconnect with her spirit guides, talk and listen intuitively to their words of wisdom. Her guides had been without speaking to her ad now there was a rush of contact, which she had to control.

She had yet to get used to the fact she had a room just for sleeping, the bed had been far too soft when she tried to rest the first night. She had to ask Oskar to have the sleeping pad removed. He had locked at her with astonishment and assumed she did not like the quality of the pad, but then he realized, she would be more comfortable sleeping on the wooden planks that supported the sleeping pad than any pad placed on them and had the pad removed immediately. There was the room for dressing in which she was now, and an opulent room for bathing. The entire building with all its attachments and other rooms, kitchens and guardhouse was walled and heavily protected.

During the second Moon Rise she had alarmed the NighT Guards by being out amongst the plantings, they were used to being alone during Moon Rise and had never had someone to guard who was down on their knees pressing ground soil around a young planting or who regularly carried heavy casks of river liquid as if they were nothing more than a roll of clothes.

There was an outdoor shower, nothing like the shower at home this was more like the one in the plantings at the monastery; she preferred a corner near where the young plantings were set out in small casks to get their first growth before going to the main garden. She would stand naked in a large cask of river liquid and use the scoop she used out in the garden to let liquid dribble over her hair, face and body; just as she had in the fields at the monastery after tending to the plantings. She could appreciate the luxury of having hot and cold liquid delivered at the turn of a knob inside, but to shower out in the plantings under full Moon Rise, the liquid had never seemed cold, even when the ground was frozen hard and snow had to be cleared from the winter strong plantings.

Oskar was at the centre of a whirlwind of activity; he and the High Protector had caught several Imperial spies at another barrier taking explosives into the generation house with the goal of destroying it and bringing down the barrier to flood the lands below it. Herbs had been administered to make them talk and they had all referred to Callar, as being the instigator and designer of their plan but local agents and thieves and robbers were responsible for carrying it out. The same herbs, but much stronger, had been administered to Callar who had eventually confessed the Emperor had personally sent him north to create groups of disaffected people from anyone he could fine and who would carry out tasks such as bring down a barrier. It was through the Emperor's agents that Lovan had been told his brother was dead.

These meetings had been conducted in another room she had, with tables and chairs, maps and plentiful lighting globes in case the needed to meet during Moon Rise. There were no windows in that room. Oskar had said he had made sure of this, he told her that if she could see Moon Rise, her knew she would leave to be with her plantings. They had laughed, but as she looked at the windowless room, she knew what he said to be true.

A cloth of intricate darkness had been unraveling before Oskar's eyes and he enjoyed his task of pulling at lose threads as they appeared and unraveling the cloth. As he pulled at a thread here or there, another revealed itself. Pendal surprised herself with her understanding of motivation and human weakness that allowed disaffected people turn into agents of disruption and destruction. Time and again she had delved into the deep darkness of this or that person to help bring more of the web into Day Rise so Oskar could see it for what it was and take action.

Then she would retreat, mediate, gain strength, and focus.

Lenvar, the Dekar-sa Empress was a revelation. Although the cord that fed Pendal in the womb had been cut and withered away many cycles ago, there was a strong connection, one that had been dormant and resting peacefully for a long time. It was now awake and Pendal found it very pleasing.

And she would train. She would train until she puked.

Oskar and the High Protector had arranged for Pendal to train with the elite of VodaKhan forces. At first they had been unhappy at the idea of training with a priest but within the first session she had crushed all sent against her and continued to train until bile forced its way out of her body. Training was not just physical it seemed to add an edge to her mental focus. She could feel clarity in her mind and mental attention that matched those special moments during Moon Rise when the air was so clear and pure that it made the moons seems to appear to be just an arms length away. All the features of the moons was clear and crisp, the greys and blues of the lower regions merged with the browns and blacks of the mountains, they hung there in the sky, inviting, casting their pure glow across the land, a glow that seemed to reveal all, and to cleanse all.

Then there was title – not a name, she had a name, Pendal. The end.

The other things she was now called, some described her, and some of them were simply there so that others had a point of reference.

She was a priest, the end.

Her name and the role of priest defined her; she had lived all her life as Pendal and preparing and practicing to be a priest. The day the monastery doors closed behind her that last time, she stood there as a priest in all but title.

She was a Blade Smith, also, the end.

From the time she was eight cycles old and had her first training session, which was also the first session she bled at the hands of a trainer, she had been learning to be adept at carrying and using her blades and at ways to fight and kill without blades that made her physical from, her body, a deadly weapon.

She was known by so many other names now, now she was the Dekar-na Empress, the Empress to be.

Just because she was her mother's daughter, she became this other regal person that and all that it meant.

Pendal checked the freedom to draw her front and back blades and checked each for razor sharpness. One of the things the NighT Guardian had done before she left was alter her blade sheaths. Each blade edge now sat between two fine stripes of a strange stone that could sharpen a blade simply by rubbing against it. As Pendal drew a blade or put it back, the blade was sharpened. But knowing that did not stop her from checking that her blades were as sharp as possible. Pendal looked up at herself in the looking glass, her back blade still in her left hand and a wry smile spread across her face, she had started thinking about her name and role as the Dekar-na Empress but the Blade Smith in her decided it was more important and severed her other thoughts.

Pendal was a healer; she could connect with the spirit and energy of another and read it and balance it or direct it somewhere for the others good.

Then a voice said in her head "you are a traveller."

Pendal slipped her blade back in its sheath and looked at her face and then her boots. Yes, she was a traveller. Her face had been covered in salty tasting liquid from a storm on the Great Salt Sea and where Emperors before her had marched their legions riding on horses or in carriages, she had walked and run. And, she had swum naked in a cold extremely clear lake when she crossed into VodaKhan. She had experienced the nature of the places she had been.

Simply by being the Dekar-Na Empress she became a senior senator, a Senator Khan in the hierarchy of the VodaKhan senate.

The senate was not in session and Oskar had taken her to the ornate building and shown her where she would sit, she sat there listening to him pointing out where different officials sat and stood when speaking she had sat and listened. But, as with the sleeping arrangements she had then as with her bed, she had complained at the softness of the seat and asked Oskar to arrange for the cushions to be removed, she would sit on the planks underneath the soft padding.

Oskar pointed out that she would then be sitting too low for the importance of her role and others would not be able to see her clearly. Pendal had been surprised that this was important; especially when Oskar said that even if she were not there the world of the senate would continue without her. Pendal had eventually replied that if it were important for people to be able to see her, she would stand. He had stared at his feet and made circles in the push carpet with his stick. That he had told her was not really the answer because if she stood, everyone else in the senate would have to stand also. Some, he laughed were too old and fat to stand for very long. They had stood in front of her chair for several moments and then she had placed her hand to his face and told him about the lake were she had swum and a rock she had crawled out on that seemed to be comfortable.

Oskar seized on the information with great energy and said he would have the rock removed and shaped so that she could again sit on it, this time in the senate. They stared at each other for a long while and then burst out laughing as they walked away. Pendal would in deed be a very different Senator Khan.

A tap at the door, Lenvar, her mother entered. She, Oskar and the High Protector were the only ones allowed to enter without one of the guards outside checking to see if who was visiting could be admitted.

Pendal came out from her dressing room and smiled warmly at her mother, "what do you think, it was completed last night and delivered this morning?" she asked.

Lenvar looked at her daughter, for the first time in her life she had a warm sense of love, happiness and pride that she had birthed the girl standing in front of her. The act of birthing was a moment of great joy and happiness, but now to see her grown and recognized as the exceptional spirit she was made her very happy. Pendal had grown to be something she could never imagine. But as she looked at her daughter there was a pang of worry and concern. "Pendal, you look immaculate, you bring liquid to my eyes, I am so proud of you, it will go well today, it can go no other way." She would have reached out and hugged Pendal but now their roles; their positions, forbade such personal contact.

Pendal had strongly resisted this block to personal contact but Lenvar said that is how she was brought up and that is how she would prefer they conduct themselves. Pendal had not contested Lenvar's words or wanted to hurt her feelings so she had agreed to follow her mother's wishes but under protest. Pendal had spoken to Oskar about it. He understood Pendal's feelings but said that if that was the way the Dekar-sa Empress wanted it that was the way it had to be. Pendal's cold response was that things would change when she became Empress, besides the prohibition against personal contact had to do with assassination, as she wore a full suit of body armour and was a Blade Smith, even if someone got too close and threatened her, they would not live long.

Oskar had agreed, she was very different from the time and person who created the protocol. But he asked, if a time, an unthinkable time should occur when the Dekar-sa Empress was a threat to Pendal, would she be able to kill her? Pendal had stiffened visibly at the question. After years of being alone she had found her mother and her father, and enjoyed both of them immensely. She had thought about it but a vice inside her said, "Yes, if you have to." She realized it was part of her life's journey something painful her spirit might have to learn as part of its growth and existence for the next life. She had told Oskar, that yes, if the time came, she could kill Lenvar. Oskar had believed her.

There was another knock at the door, Oskar and the High Protector entered. They were dressed with restrained elegance and with the trappings of their offices and rank.

Lenvar as the Dekar-sa Empress if not in speech, manners, or dress should overshadow Pendal, the Dekar-na Empress but as Pendal was wearing the colours of a priest there was very little she could wear that did not. The Dekar-sa Empress was dressed in the sandy, earthy colours of the work robes she had worn the day she had first met Pendal.

As Oskar opened his mouth to speak the Dekar-sa Empress made a funny chirping sound! Pendal looked at her mother with astonishment.

"Your fingers, your nails, you have ground soil under them!" she pointed at Pendal's hands as he exclaimed the information.

Pendal looked down at her hands, her fingers and her nails which had been so carefully preened just days before. "I was out planting at Third Moon Rise, of course there ground soil!" she looked at her mother, "and of course I know, I am not allowed it." With a casual nonchalance, Pendal reached behind and pulled out her back blade, twirled it in her left hand until she was gripping the blade close to the tip. "Now, please, tell me again?" Within a few seconds the ground soil was gone from three of her fingernails, she became aware of the silence and looked up at the three of them staring at her hands. "What?" she asked.

The High Protector looked up and met her gaze. "Its just that I have never seen someone so casual and yet certain with such a weapon as deadly as that blade."

Pendal just shrugged, and changed hands with the blade to clean the nails on her other hand.

"Dekar-na Empress, Senator Khan, Pendal. This will be the first session of the senate you will attend. You have met several Senators; they have all been highly impressed with you and have spread the word. Your exploits as a Blade Smith and traveller are almost legendary now. You need say nothing, but if you do wish to say something…. I suggest you do not. There is a gold rod at the end of the right arm of your seat. Simply lift it and you will have immediate attention of the Senate. Anyone who is speaking must stop and surrender the senate floor to you." Oskar took a deep breath and bowed, and so did the High Protector.

Pendal looked at the back of Oskar's head and so to the back of the High Protectors head, Even her mother was held stationary in a slightly deferential bow.

"I understand and will not say anything that would affect the moment. And, all of you raise your heads and look me in the eyes." Pendal had finished cleaning her nails and slipped the blade back into its sheath. She held out her hands to her mother and wiggled her fingers, "are they are clean now?" she asked.

Her mother smiled and nodded.

"Well I am glad we can agree my nails are clean of ground soil and look presentable. And the bowing will stop; it does not show me any deference because I do not ask for it. I will let you know when I feel I have earned it. If I need you to bow so I can make sure you have had your hair trimmed and cleaned with some good soap, I will ask. Never, ever, bow to me again."

Oskar started to open his mouth and the High protector looked as he too were about to say something about protocol or something, but Pendal continued, "Oskar my friend, you mentioned two titles and my name when you addressed me just now," she nodded and Oskar responded with a nod. "I am a priest, that comes before all other titles does not? It even comes before Dekar-na Empress." she nodded again at Oskar and he responded. "Blade Smith as a title, comes before my name," she nodded again at Oskar and he responded. She reached out and stroked his face and squeezed his shoulders.

The opening of the VodaKhan senate was like nothing Pendal had seen or heard before. All around, the bright blaring of trumpets and horns, and the banging and rhythmic pulsing of drums and banners everywhere.

The VodaKhan senate unlike the ones in the lower regions had a combination of hereditary members, elected, and trade members. As each new member entered the aisle between the banked rows of those present their title and name would be announced loudly to the all present. Beside them, walked a barer carrying the banner for him or her. The banner matched one of the groups with whom they would sit. Where in the group they sat indicated their status within the group. Higher at the back the less important, closer to the front, the more important, this was especially important for the elected members.

Music played according to the request of each new member.

Pendal was the last to enter; ritual indicated that none could follow all must precede her.

Her banner was as maroon as her robes and edged with blue and gold braided rope. Inside the rope edging it had an intense black band the width of her main blade indicating her status as a Blade Smith. On the inner maroon square, it carried sacred symbols denoting her Order and her priest hood.

She had requested no music, not because she did not know any that should be played, which was true, but because similar ceremonies at the monastery, when they all gathered together to honour someone were done in silence. Pendal wanted that tradition and the lack of sound, to be a mark of her entrance on to the stage of the Senate. For her there would be no bombastic music, fanfares or ritual music. Silence would have an enormous impact.

Silence sat across the senate like a vacuum over their ears. Not a sound was made as she walked slowly, matching the pace of her banner barer to her seat. Her seat she was pleased to see was no longer stuffed with opulent cushions but the stone Oskar had said he would have transported for her to sit on. It had been finely worked and polished to an incredible sheen. As she looked down at it for the first time she was surprised to see veins of ore that were maroon, blue, and gold, at the edge, the edges were black. Her colours.

Pendal possessed immense power and influence; she would sit with no one.

She sat down and took in the scene of more than a hundred faces turned toward her. In the gallery reserved for officials and government dignitaries, her mother looked down beaming with pride. Oskar and the High protector looked down with a mixture of pride and the realization that very soon life would change for all, in VodaKhan as well as the lower regions, the Dekar-na Empress was now revealed.